ALSO BY P. G. STURGES

Shortcut Man

TRIBULATIONS OF THE
SHORTCUT MAN

a novel

p. g. sturges

SCRIBNER

New York   London   Toronto   Sydney   New Delhi

SCRIBNER
A Division of Simon & Schuster, Inc.
1230 Avenue of the Americas
New York, NY 10020

First Scribner hardcover edition February 2012

SCRIBNER and design are registered trademarks of The Gale Group, Inc. used under license by Simon & Schuster, Inc., the publisher of this work.

For information about special discounts for bulk purchases, please contact Simon & Schuster Special Sales at 1-866-506-1949 or business@simonandschuster.com

The Simon & Schuster Speakers Bureau can bring authors to your live event. For more information or to book an event, contact the Simon & Schuster Speakers Bureau at 1-866-248-3049 or visit our website at www.simonspeakers.com.

Manufactured in the United States of America

10 9 8 7 6 5 4 3 2 1

Library of Congress Control Number is available.

ISBN 978-1-4391-9421-8
ISBN 978-1-4391-9423-2 (ebook)

Dedicated to:

Mac, Kelly, Taka, Thomas, Sam, and Kian

A Note from the Author

It is not the author's intention to amend, emend, reduce, ameliorate, or redress any wrongs, misfortunes, tragedies, or perditious conditions known to exist in this world or the next. You will depart the premises no wiser than you arrived. However, it is hoped you will be entertained in the meantime.

Contents

CONTENTS

Part Two: Bambi Service

CONTENTS

Part Three: Public Property

PART ONE

Goodbye to All That

CHAPTER ONE

White Fools with Dreadlocks

Loman London believed the labors of others should profit Loman London. I had been summoned to disabuse him, again, of this quaint notion.

A soft Los Angeles morning sun gentled my shoulders as I made a left turn in my '69 Cadillac Coupe de Ville convertible from Ocean Avenue to Abbot Kinney Boulevard.

Kiyoko was on my mind. My on-and-off girlfriend, Kiyoko was a Buddhist who hadn't yet come to appreciate my line of work. Last night, to the accompaniment of Japanese imprecations, she'd thrown me out of her house. It didn't help that I'd laughed at her insults. I couldn't help it. I understood only a few words of Japanese. *Forku, porku, steaku, elephanto.* Americanized additions to the language. Not the words she had chosen from the other side of the kitchen island. So I laughed, hoping to bluff my way through; a sitcom, a new take on the Odd Couple.

Exiled. One arm stiffly pointing in the direction of the Pacific Ocean, she summed up her aggravations in one word: *barbarian.*

Up ahead on the left was my morning's destination, a modern, two-story, yellow stucco building with purposely protruding I-beams. It housed the Peach Cat & Dog Hospital and heralded the gentrification of funky Venice. I parked in back and got out.

The thing was this: Kiyoko believed all human suffering sprang from the denial of death. That denial took the form of greed, anger, and foolishness. And I agreed. Hell, I couldn't agree more. But before everybody wised up there'd be problems here and there. That's my line. My name's Dick Henry. They call me the Shortcut Man.

Clark Peach, wringing his hands, met me at the back door. Clark was five foot seven, weighed all of a hundred and twenty pounds, peered at the world through delicate gold-rimmed spectacles. He was one of the premier veterinarians in Los Angeles, according to a magazine that evaluated stuff like that. Ferocious, intractable beasts became docile in his presence. I'd seen that. But people? People were a different kind of beast.

"Thanks for coming, Dick."

I liked him a lot. He'd actually done something useful with his life. "You the man, Dr. Peach," I slanged. "Whazzup?"

Of course, I had a good idea what was up.

Dr. Peach kicked an invisible piece of dirt on the floor, then looked up. "Uh, he's, uh, he's back."

I nodded. Dr. Peach was at the butt end of a low-level extortion scam perpetrated by Loman London.

I'd told London to go away early last week. "I didn't see him on my way in, Doc."

Dr. Peach checked his watch. "He'll be here anytime now."

"Why didn't you call me sooner?"

The doctor shrugged, with a tinge of embarrassment. "I, uh, I thought maybe I could talk to him myself."

Hence my vocation.

Doc Peach beckoned to me to follow him. He walked into his office, looked out through the blinds. He turned to me, nodded.

I took a look for myself.

Loman London was a fiftyish wastrel whose contributions to society had not yet added up to a popcorn fart. Two hundred seventy or so pounds were apportioned over his large frame with a hefty surplus accumulating at the waistline. Matted dreadlocks depended thickly to his shoulders. His skin was rough and permanently reddened. Treelike legs, in shorts, interfaced the pavement through a pair of huaraches.

Loman's scam was a simple one. He would set up his rolling incense cart in front of a likely business and wait to be paid to go somewhere else. In the meantime he would frighten the little blue-haired old ladies bringing their little blue poodles in for a checkup.

I turned to the doc. "I guess Mr. London has a learning disability. I'll go out and have a talk with him."

But first I retrieved an accelerant from the Caddy's trunk. I walked around the building. Tendrils of pungent smoke rose from the incense stand into the morning air. I actually liked the smell. Rastaman greeted me in friendly fashion.

"Salutations, mon. What's your pleasure? Sandalwood or Pondi-cherry Pine?" Loman spoke in a pseudo-Jamaican patois.

I stared at him for a second. Beneath his sunny innocence was a surly streak. "I thought we discussed this, pal. You were going to exhibit elsewhere."

"And I did, mon. That was last week. This is this week."

The "mon" shit irritated me all over again. Loman the lump hadn't been within a thousand miles of Jamaica. Though I was sure he'd smoked ten thousand spliffs. On someone else's dime.

"Doctor Peach isn't going to pay you again. He asks that you move on."

There I was. The soul of reason. Even though I had just begun to feel that peculiar tingling in my fists.

Rastaman shrugged. "And I have entertained his request, mon. Dr. Peach a good mon. But I have found a home for my business. This is a free country, mon."

"The doctor patiently asks you to move on."

Rastaman shrugged with a hint of brusqueness. "I have found a home for my business, mon."

"And you refuse to listen to reason." I was giving bad Bob Marley a last chance. I imagined the I-Three's shaking their heads in unison behind him. Of course, London wasn't appreciating his opportunity.

"I refuse to be intimidated, if that's what you mean, mon." He folded his thick arms over his thick chest. His friendliness had evaporated.

His chin was calling to my knuckles, but, thinking of Kiyoko, I hung on a little longer. "I guess you don't recognize the former light-heavyweight champion of the Thirteenth Naval District."

"Should I be worried, mon?"

It was the "mon" that did it. I stepped around his wares, planted my left foot, launched a right uppercut. The karma missile caught him on the point of the chin and set him, with a thud, flatly on his ass, knocking the wind out of him.

I reached into my back pocket for the can of Ronsonol Lighter Fluid and soaked down the entire incense stand.

Rastaman had not yet regained his feet. He shook his head as if to clear it.

Having survived some righteous shots both in and out of the ring, I knew what he was experiencing. He was hearing a great swarm of bees, though he could not see them.

I indicated his stand. "You ever get your schnoz into what these things smell like when they're all burning at once?"

I patted down my pockets with a theatrical flair. Had I really forgotten my lighter?

Awareness slowly crept into Rastaman's face. He looked at his incense stand, then the yellow Ronsonol can.

"Does anyone have a match around here?" I laid my request before the universe.

Rastaman held up a belaying hand.

But the universe saw fit to reply.

"I got a match, brother."

My heart warmed. I turned and there was Rojas, right on schedule. "Enrique Montalvo Rojas! As I live and breathe!"

Artfully chapeaued in black porkpie, Enrique Rojas was a badass Eastsider. An old colleague with a supremely checkered past, he had romanced heroin, done a stretch at San Quentin, and had found a cat's-eye worth a million dollars in Sri Lanka that currently supported an orphanage or two. He bore a passionate love for Eric Dolphy and Thelonius Monk.

Rojas eyed the stand. "Should I light it on fire?"

I smiled. "Please."

From the sidewalk Rastaman waved his hand. "Whoa, now. That's my entire stock, there, man." Man, not *mon*.

I indicated Rojas. "This is Señor Rojas. Señor Rojas loves to beat the shit out of white fools with dreadlocks. Especially ones trying to shake down veterinarians in Venice. Have I made myself clear?"

Rastaman now grasped the full breadth of his misapprehension. "I get it, man. Real clear. Don't burn my shit. I got places to go. Please."

Rojas lit a match. "Shall we give the dude another chance?"

"Please," begged Loman the lump.

I feigned consideration.

"One more chance?" queried Rojas again, appearing for a second to be a nice guy.

"Uhhh . . ." I watched London hang on my every word. ". . . uhh, nah." I shook my head. "Light him up."

"Okay," said Rojas, bubbling with good cheer. He tossed the match onto the stand and it went up in a huge whoosh of flame and wave of heat.

"Thank you, Señor Rojas." I bowed low.

"Thank you, Señor Henry." Rojas bowed in return.

CHAPTER TWO

Billy Hitler

After a ride north and some quick stir-fry at Hoy's Wok, I rolled over to World Book & News at Hollywood and Cahuenga. Jack Hathaway did a five-day ten-to-six and took messages for me. Jack was a Navy veteran in his seventies, a cheerful man with a ready smile and a pirate squint. The failings of humanity, from Genghis Khan to Billy Hitler, never clouded his fundamental optimism for long.

Khan had skewered a million sobbing virgins. Hitler, a clumsy shoplifter of Jack's acquaintance, self-appellated in the style of Sid Vicious, sold 213 copies of his CD, worldwide, and had gone on to OD in the men's room of the Pig 'n Whistle on Hollywood Boulevard.

Informed of Hitler's demise, Jack had shaken his head. "They *allow* that? At the Pig 'n Whistle? And that rat still owed me money." Then he shrugged. "But whatcha gonna do? We have to go on."

I agreed. Like other misfortunes outside the direct sphere of my concern, I met the news of young Hitler's passing with great resolve. Hitler's previous handle had been Sparky Wire. And the Rubber Gloves. But amphetamines had disagreed with his spleen. The Gloves slowly disintegrated without him.

I put a hand on Jack's shoulder. "You said I had some messages."

Jack grinned. "I think I got a gig for you." He reached into his pocket, put a card in my hand. "Take a look at this."

Judge Harry Glidden
Superior Court

I seemed to recognize the name. "Have I heard of this guy?"

"Everybody has, Dick. That's Hangin' Harry."

Hangin' Harry Glidden. The real judge who'd done some TV then married a cable-channel lady chef. Or whatever she was. "What'd he want?"

Jack shook his head. "Wouldn't tell *me* nothin', of course. Wanted you." Then Jack remembered something else. "And there's been a kid coming by."

"A kid?"

"Fifteen, sixteen."

"Someone steal his bicycle?"

"He wouldn't tell me nothin', either." Jack grinned. "Maybe he's gonna be a judge."

"Maybe. But I don't deal with kids. You know that."

"Told him that. But he keeps comin' back. Came back yesterday."

"Asked for me?"

"Yesiree. For Mister Dick Henry."

I didn't deal with kids. Or snakes.

Jack ran an eye over his racks, then glanced up into the mirrors that looked down on the aisles. "Hell, Dick. There he is now." He pointed into the mirror.

A kid was checking out something in the masked avenger section.

"You Dick Henry?"

"Yeah. But listen, kid. I don't do stuff for kids. It's a legal thing."

The boy was tall and skinny. Serious eyes. "What I wanted to talk to you about was—"

I cut him right off. "Don't waste your breath on me. I don't work for kids. No exceptions. You got school counselors, campus police, after-school clubs, a thousand people to turn to. Sorry. No exceptions. Good luck."

I turned to Jack, waved. "Catch you later, Jack. Thanks." I turned to the kid. "Good luck, son."

I could feel the kid's eyes on my back as I walked down Cahuenga. You gotta draw a line.

CHAPTER THREE

Classical Dance

Art Lewis lived in his dream house up Temescal Canyon off Pacific Coast Highway. He was seventy-four years old, six foot four, two-forty, a big, broad-chested man with a full, natural head of white hair. He'd fought and pushed and scratched and now he was done with the struggle. He'd made his money. He'd taken care of those it had fallen his lot to take care of. Now he did what he pleased.

What pleased him was Pussy Grace.

Pussy was a stripper of heroic and perfect dimension. Blond, blue-eyed, in her thirty-second year, she was not witless, but she was not an economist either. She was endearingly fallible, and possessed of a sunny disposition that made time in her company well spent. She had a little of her own money and she was not greedy. She was happy to be with Art and he was happy to take care of her. One day flew into the next.

Art liked to cook, and was doing so now, adding chopped onions to the small, copper-bottomed fry pan where garlic and cilantro were liquefying in virgin olive oil. He adjusted the flame down a bit. Copper transmitted heat quickly.

"Remind me, Puss. We need some more extra-virgin olive oil."

Pussy smiled up at him. "I used to be a virgin. But I was never an extra virgin."

"Who needs extra virgins? I'm not a schoolboy. I like experience."

"You know I don't have much of that." She checked her watch again.

"Nervous?"

"Jesus, Art, I'm not used to *meeting* judges. I'm used to standing in front of them."

He threw his head back and laughed in that big bark of his.

"You're going to be just fine. You're here because I want you here. And the judge? The judge is a man whose dad could afford to send his son to law school. No better than you and me, certainly."

"I know we're all the same before God and that stuff. But we're not before God. I'm a stripper, Art."

Art beamed down on her. "And that's just one of the reasons I like you. I got fifty others." He patted her ass with one of his huge hands.

She was still doubtful. "O-kay." She brushed a few more cilantro leaves into the mix.

"Bottom line, Puss, remember why the judge is here."

"Tell me again."

"Money. Like any cook, sign painter, valet parker, or wedding violinist, he wants money. For some cockamamie scheme."

"What are you going to tell him?"

"The same thing I tell everyone else. *No.*"

"I like that word."

"What word?"

"Cockamamie."

Good God. She was still beautiful. Those eyes. And that smile. Sin and salvation. He'd watched her so long on television it was almost like he had known her. Then they met.

"I'm Judge Glidden."

"I'm Ellen Havertine."

She'd liked him. Really liked him. Laughed at his jokes. Touched his arm when they were talking on the set.

Touching is not a lie. That was one of his maxims. Physical contact between a man and a woman of appropriate age was never an accident. It happened or it didn't. Even down to the seemingly incidental, two people at the office coffee mess, a woman didn't even bump elbows or allow herself contact with someone she was specifically uninterested in.

Their conversations had been vivid and wide-ranging. Her knowledge of the law was surprisingly deep.

"Of course, I'm not a lawyer," she'd laughed, "but I play one on TV."

"Or you stayed in a Holiday Inn," he rejoined cleverly.

"You'd have to do better than a Holiday Inn if you wanted me in a hotel, Judge."

A frozen moment. Then he jumped in with both feet.

"What about the Island? In Newport?"

"I prefer the Balboa Bay."

That was the exact moment he, the Honorable Harold J. Glidden, had allowed the fracture of his old life. Invited the fracture.

I like the Balboa, too.

A week after *Law & Order* had wrapped, that's where they had spent a couple of days. And nights.

How had he put it to Patricia? Miss Havertine and her representation wanted to consult him, for, uh, his legal expertise, uh, as a background, a background for creating a new cable series. About a lawyer, a female lawyer, a female lawyer in the dog-eat-dog world of Los Angeles law.

Over the course of that weekend Ellen had taken him places he'd never been, places beyond his dreams. With horror he realized he'd been drifting sleepily toward the end of his life, hypnotized by the road, unaware there were still significant journeys yet to be undertaken. Ellen had woken him up.

If he were down to the last chapters of his life, he decided he would live it his way. He'd made enough money to be comfort-able, he'd raised his kids, he'd seen Patricia through everything. But Patricia had settled for old age and, after time with Ellen, he just couldn't do that. So, with due responsibility, he'd chucked every-thing and endured the scandal.

He'd felt young again, naked, exposed, alive. So *alive*. His chil-dren, Todd and Monica, had been furious with him. But he'd expected that. Loyalty to their mother. It was natural. They weren't in his shoes. Christ, like that old cliché, he had shoes older than they were. They couldn't possibly understand what a man felt as he gazed into the sunset. Gazed into the sunset bored stiff.

He'd been generous to Patricia. Who'd spurned his offer of con-tinuing friendship, who'd barely said another word to him since. The woman scorned. She'd dragged her feet through every evolu-tion, every procedure, and at the bitter end, tenaciously fought for one of the few things she knew he'd grown to love.

A painting. *Kostabi #5.* She hadn't kept it physically, but she'd retained legal ownership of it. Bitch.

A month after the divorce he'd married Ellen in grand and public style. He'd been in all those magazines at the checkout stand.

He and Ellen had actually gone on to create a show. *Ellen Hayes, Special Counsel.* With that, and his recurring role on *Law & Order,* he had turned into a real celebrity. A celebrity judge. On the *cover* of all those magazines at the supermarket. Featured alongside murder-ers, thieves, and betrayers bereft of makeup, enflabbed at the beach.

The only trouble with being a celebrity was acting like one. Wav-ing like a grandee, smiling with his newly veneered teeth, pretend-ing age was just a number. Spending lavishly, traveling first class, entertaining new friends. Tipping waiters, tipping parking boys, tipping anyone with a heartbeat. Anyone who might tattle to a tab-loid, leak to the Internet. *That Judge Glidden is one tight-ass son of a bitch.*

After a while even Monica and Todd had come to believe he was having a ball. And he was. You know, pretty much.

For four years he'd kept all the glittering balls in the air. Then, after acrimonious negotiations, in which he had been sure to prevail, *Special Counsel* had been canceled. With an abrupt income loss of $65,000 a week. But the celebrity train kept right on rolling. Other deals, sure things, scribed in stone, disappeared like tarpaper shacks in a hurricane. He recalled something Hemingway had said about going broke. *Slowly at first, then all at once.*

The lights of the 7 series BMW played across the wrought-iron gates of Art Lewis's place. His window whispered down and he reached out, pressed the green key on the entry pad.

Ellen stabbed out her cigarette. "What's this woman's name again?"

"I'm not sure. Kitty. Prissy. Something like that."

"Prissy? *I don't know nothin' 'bout birthin' no babies, Miss Scarlett.* That's Prissy."

"Maybe I got it wrong. She's a stripper, for godsake. Like all his girlfriends."

"She could be highly cultured."

"You're right. Maybe she plays the piano."

"Or the skin flute."

They both laughed, then they heard someone key the intercom and then Art's voice. "Who is it?"

He'd always admired Art's voice. Low, sandpaper rough, gruff, no fooling around. "It's Harry and Ellen," said Harry.

"Ellen and Harry," said Art, smiling through the wire, "come on in."

The big gate rolled back silently.

Art and Pussy waited in the entryway for their guests.

"So *don't* introduce you as Pussy."

16

"Don't you *dare*. Not to people like these people. I told you what to call me."

Ellen had just repaired her lipstick when the front door opened. There was Art and his stripper. Firm and high. Store-bought. Woman looked terrified. Probably Harry's effect. There was more to his fame than his tan. He was a sitting judge in Superior Court. Hangin' Harry Glidden.

"Come on in, folks. Come on in." Art's bad-road face splintered into a grin. "Harry and Ellen, meet one of my good friends, Miss Penelope Grace."

The judge nodded, smiled, extended a smooth hand. "Penelope. How do you do?"

Pussy took the hand, tried to be classy. "Pleased to meetcha."

"Call me Harry."

"Yes, Your Honor."

Everyone chuckled.

Good Christ. Her cultural seams were showing. Like discount stockings.

"I'm Ellen," said the movie star.

Puss took her hand and tried to smile at the same time. "I'm Puh-nelope," she said, almost blowing it.

It was going to be an informal dinner. In the kitchen. Thank God. There were too many knives and forks in the dining room. The judge and his wife were escorted to the big peasant table, set festively, with candles. A window looked out on the fountain and the pond. Art put a real log in the fireplace.

The meal hadn't started well. The judge got off the line with some heavy shit about marketplace ethics and ended up at the opera downtown.

Pussy looked narrowly at Art, knowing this would happen. *Marketplace ethics*. She shopped at MarketBasket, they seemed honest enough. And, Christ, she didn't know crap about opera. Someone named Gary was either an architect or a composer and whatever it was he had done was a masterpiece. Big deal. Then someone named Mickey built it. The judge turned to her with his blinding teeth. Had she been to the hall?

The hall. Uh, no, at least she didn't think so. But she was planning to. Soon. Real soon. She loved the hall. The judge and the special counsel bitch just nodded their perfect heads.

She was utterly at sea and clutched her wine for flotation. Then Art said he'd seen enough opera to last a lifetime in one long weekend in Italy, in one of those bullshit cities. Florence, that was it. Which meant flowers, right? Art liked jazz. Pepper. He dug Art Pepper.

Then the wine kicked in and everything was alright. She'd deflected questions about her former career but Special Counsel had gotten the wrong idea.

"So . . . you've moved on from classical dance."

"Uh . . . yes," said Puss. Classical pole dancing. But why should she feel down? She'd read about Miss Special Counsel more than once in the tabloids. Miss Havertine had lassoed a few poles here and there. Including the judge's. Men were utterly predictable.

Art surveyed his guests, smiled. Pussy had been magnificent. Keeping the conversational denominator low enough to prevent the judge from shoveling his rich, high-falutin' manure. Art. Literature. Economics. That dismal superstition.

Fucking economics. The only time Art was sure that Pussy had seen the *Wall Street Journal* was in the bottom of Tinkerbell's cage. Until Tinkerbell had flown into a wall and broken her neck. Parakeets were stupid.

Pussy related the triple play they'd seen last week at Chavez Ravine. With two out in the sixth inning.

At that point the judge threw in the towel.

"A fantastic meal, Art. Really great," said the judge, formally setting his fork down. Conversation was an art, impossible to practice in the company of the disenfranchised.

"And the remodel," Ellen looked around the kitchen, "it looks so good. What I've seen of it."

"Why, thank you, Ellen." Art beamed, wiped his mouth, set his napkin aside. He turned to Pussy. "Puss, why don't you give Ellen the grand tour while I have a cigar with Harry?"

As Pussy showed Special Counsel the house, she realized Miss High Life wasn't really so bad once you got to know her a little.

"Art called you Puss?"

"Uh . . . like Puss in Boots."

"I thought it might be short for Penelope."

"That, too." Puss gestured around the kitchen. She would start the tour here. "This, as you can see, is the kitchen. Biggest kitchen I've ever been in."

"It is big."

She pointed to the cooking island. "And here's the stove, a twelve-burner Jenn-Air right here in the middle. And here, four restaurant ovens, two on each side. Up to five hundred degrees," she added helpfully. "And up there are the smoke fans."

"Smoke fans," said Ellen. Had Art invited the pole dancer to keep Harry off balance? So he could more easily turn him down?

Puss stopped in front of two huge stainless-steel walk-in freezers. "Art put these in special. Walk-in freezers. Big enough to walk right in."

"You mean actual walk-in *walk-in* freezers."

"That's what I mean."

"Remarkable." She'd gone over the presentation with Harry. They already had soft money. But who didn't? What they needed was five million in cash. And the distribution—they'd get distribution, no worries.

The pole dancer pointed out a strange, skinny door. "This is what Art calls the security shack."

In the library, sixty-five feet away, wreathed in the smoke of two fine Upmann cigars, Art nodded contemplatively.

Glidden wanted him to invest in a movie that would lead to a cable series. The movie seemed strong. Some action, some sex, some cars. And Ellen still looked good. But what the hell did Art Lewis know about movies? Just enough to get fucked.

Long ago he'd learned the hard way that you never went into a business you didn't know absolutely everything about. Like he knew screw threads. Fasteners, translation, gear reduction, measurement. He knew everything there was to know about screws and threads. Plug gages. Tapered plugs. *Handbook H-28.* He knew it in and out, chapter and verse. But movies? *Gone With the Wind* still hadn't made a goddamn profit. Not to worry. It had only been seventy years.

He looked up into Harry's eyes. Harry would find someone or something else. "My answer is no, Harry. With regret, but no, just the same." Of course, a man with money never said yes at the first request. Otherwise he would no longer be a man with money.

In the security shack Puss pointed at all the video screens. Didn't look like the system was on. Underneath them a computer whirred and there were wires going everywhere. "I don't know how all this stuff works, I'm not oriented, technically, uh, you know. But Art says you can see a gnat's ass for twenty-four hours or something like that."

"Fascinating," said Ellen. Maybe Harry was shaking hands with Art right now, victorious.

Harry stood up, masking his disappointment with nonchalance. "Art, thanks for the straight shooting. I appreciate it. And Ellen appreciates it. And we appreciate the opportunity to run it by you."

Harry extended his hand and it disappeared into Art's big mitt. *Shit.*

The BMW moved down Pacific Coast Highway. Gloom pervaded the silence. "Son of a bitch wouldn't part with a goddamn penny."

Ellen stared out into the ocean, exhaled her cigarette smoke into the slipstream. "Her name is Pussy. Pussy Grace."

CHAPTER FOUR

Kostabi #5

My car, my '69 Caddy Coupe de Ville, was nearly forty years old. But that was okay. I was driving through Angeleno Heights, where the houses were a hundred years old. I was headed downtown, to the Pantry, at Ninth and Figueroa.

If you didn't love the Pantry, you didn't love L.A. With the exception of one sad, single day in the mid-'90s, the Pantry had been open, continually, 24/7, since 1929. Never without a customer. My father had been a customer. Now he and all the pretty girls he had chased were dust on top of every window blind in the city. Not that I did a lot of dusting.

I parked across the street, walked over, got a seat toward the back. The Pantry had a full crew of union waiters, all male and professional. I liked watching them work. Not one out-of-work actor among them. Coleslaw and French bread were quickly delivered and I set in.

I waited for Hangin' Harry. My newest prospective client. Then I looked up and there he was. Tall, craggy, white-headed, firm of jaw and white of tooth, born to the bench.

"Dick Henry?"

"That's me."

We both ordered New York steaks. He went well-done. I don't

generally trust a man who orders well-done. Can't be afraid of your meat. I go medium-rare.

I could tell he liked being a celebrity; he would turn to a glance like a pansy to the sun. We small-talked about baseball. The Dodgers had played a doubleheader and pulled a triple play or something. Big bucks, free-agency, and the new, greedy owners had worn down my loyalty to the team. Vin Scully, I loved. Everybody loved Vin.

After a bit, Judge Glidden felt comfortable enough to start in on the subject he had come for.

"People say you're a man who, uh, can handle unusual problems."

As long as they weren't my own. "Some people say that," I corrected.

"I'm hoping you're a man of discretion."

I waited.

"The bottom line is . . . I need a painting"—his rich baritone fell to just above a whisper—"I need a painting reproduced."

"Reproduced. You mean copied—in its original medium."

"That's what I mean."

"I know some people. Think we can do that."

"What kind of money are we talking about? Ballpark."

"What kind of picture? What level of quality you want?"

The judge leaned forward. "You ever hear of Kostabi?"

Kostabi took his place on the long list of celebrated persons I knew nothing about. "Who's he?"

"A modern surrealist. I own a piece of his called *Kostabi Number Five*."

"What's the copy for?"

"You need to know?"

"No. But it may help."

Glidden went silent for a second, acknowledged someone with a flash of his expensive teeth. "What do you know about me, Mr. Henry?"

I'd looked him up. "You're a Superior Court judge. I see you on TV every once in a while. You're married to an actress."

The judge shrugged his padded shoulders. "That's not inaccurate, but I sum up a little better than that. I'm also an author, a producer, and an entrepreneur." He smiled at the busboy. "I was also married before. In the divorce settlement with Patricia, Patricia got the Kostabi."

I waited.

"But I never gave it to her. I held off."

I began to get an inkling of where this was going. "Held off, or you're *holding* off."

"Holding off."

"How long?"

"Four years and some."

"Possession is nine-tenths of the law."

"But now it's down to that ten percent. I haven't given it to her because she didn't really want it. She just wanted *me* not to have it."

"But now she wants her property. For spite."

"For spite. Pure, cold, and bitter."

"Married a long time."

"Years too long."

"Your first wife."

"My first wife."

"So you want to surrender a copy. So she'll gloat over a phony."

He smiled coldly. "That's exactly what I want."

"How would you characterize your wife's knowledge of art?"

"Trivial."

"I mean your ex-wife's."

The judge laughed. "Trivial."

"How good do you want the copy to be?"

"Beyond casual professional suspicion."

"What's the painting worth today?"

"Neighborhood of thirty."

A name had leapt immediately to mind. Dennis would do it for . . . uh, for three or four grand. He could copy anything. I was never able to tell the difference. Which didn't say anything at all.

"I'm thinking ten grand. Around there."

"That's expensive."

"Kinko's'll do it for a dollar fifty."

This Dick Henry was a smart-ass. But he couldn't let Patricia have that picture. Fuck it. Money was money. He'd make more.

He pulled out his wallet, slid the Shortcut Man his card. Wonder where he'd gotten that moniker. "Call me, please, Mr. Henry. When you've got a firm figure. Thanks for your time."

We stood, shook hands.

I rolled down Figueroa, picked up 10 East. The freeway was sluggish but I was in a sunny mood. Kostani—or was it Kostabi?—whoever he was, I'd look him up on the net later. The nice thing was, through the unfathomable labyrinth of chance and circumstance, he would cause money to flow into my pocket. Sometimes it was good to be alive.

Then a call came in from Jack at World Book. A few more messages. Would I like to stop by?

Jack had three leads for me. "One of 'em a very pretty woman," he said with a pirate wink. "And that kid. He's been back."

"What does he not understand?" A rhetorical question. I *don't* work with children.

By the way. How do you turn your girlfriend into a pirate? Come in her eye, kick her in the shin. Then she's squinting and hopping. Peg-leg Pete.

"There's the kid, now," said Jack.

Don't try the pirate thing with your wife.

"Mr. Henry?"

"What did I tell you before?"

"That you don't work with kids."

"That's right. That hasn't changed." Though I did *hire* children. My Laurel Canyon Irregulars. They ran errands, followed people, climbed fences and trees, took pictures. "What's your name, son?"

"Latrell Scott."

An alarm bell rang in my chest.

"My mother is Nedra Scott."

My heart dropped through the floor.

CHAPTER FIVE

A Judge, a Doctor, a Priest

Mort Feinstein turned from the dramatic view of Los Angeles afforded by his nineteenth-floor office. He'd seen this happen many times. To actors, to producers, to stupid, pierced, green-haired musicians. But not often to a judge. Judges were supposed to be sober. But Glidden had mixed categories. Dangerous. You didn't want to hear Eddie Murphy sing. Glidden was now a celebrity judge.

The judge was looking for good news but there wasn't any. Mort held up two fingers.

"Peace?" asked Glidden, confused.

"This is not peace, Harry. This is two words."

"What two words?"

"You're broke."

A rainy night had fallen. The Charthouse on PCH was usually one of his favorite hangs. The staff knew him, always greeted him like an old friend. His picture up behind the bar.

Watch your step. Hangin' Harry Glidden.

In the photo he pointed his finger at the viewer like a pistol. One of those Western lawmen. One of those tough Western lawmen with veneered teeth.

He and Ellen were drinking Bloody Marys. He'd broken an

amended version of Feinstein's comments to her. She wasn't taking it all that well.

"Are you *broke,* Harry? Is that what you're saying?"

"No, dear. That's not what I'm saying. I'm saying that our circumstances will be a little straightened for a while, that's all."

"I don't like the sound of that."

"You might have to get used to the sound of that."

"I *won't* get used to it. I didn't marry you for straightened circumstances."

What had Benjamin Franklin said? What you wanted in times of stress: an old dog, an old wife, and ready money. An old wife. One who wouldn't be relentlessly demanding he pop a chubby and perform like a nineteen-year-old. "That's Christian of you, Ellen."

"Christian?" returned Ellen. "Who ever said I was a Christian?" She'd have to call that asshole Feinstein, see what really went down. She polished off her Bloody Mary. The bartender didn't know how to pour. She'd have to have another. She *needed* another. Then she remembered. "By the way, Ed Huff called."

"Fuck Ed Huff."

"Who *is* Ed Huff? A doctor, right?"

"He's a doctor who likes to play golf with celebrities."

"Why does he want to play with you?"

Bitch. "Thank you, dear."

"Jesus, Harry. Your skin is getting awfully thin. Tell me about Huff."

"One day we were playing a round at Riviera. I got interviewed on the green by Bill Devers of Channel Nine about ticket fixing for college athletes. Huff got a little airtime and someone gave him a blow job. He's been white on rice ever since."

Which reminded him of that interview with Constance Whitmore of Channel 13. About fairness and the Supreme Court. He'd pointed out the court didn't have to be fair, the laws just had to apply to everyone. He'd flashed his teeth and bingo, she'd sucked his dick.

He drank off his Bloody Mary. "That fucking Art Lewis. With one stroke of his pen he could've set us right."

"He's too carried away banging that stripper in the can."

"He bangs her in the can? She told you that?"

"No. But I can tell."

"Oh, shut up."

Ellen laughed, but then put a serious hand on his arm. "What if I told you a way we could get our hands on a lot of money."

The invitation to evil always came smoothly. Ah, for an old wife. "What's a lot of money?"

"Fifty million dollars."

"That's a lot of money." A shot of nausea ran through him. Maybe it was the bivalve mollusks on the half-shell. "Sounds wrong already."

"Wrong is an opinion."

"I'm paid for my opinions."

Harry *was* broke. She could feel it. She smiled in that pissed-off way, shrugged her shoulders. "Fine. End of subject." She picked up her menu, pretended to study it. "I'll have the surf 'n' turf, dear. *If we can afford it.*"

She knew he couldn't take a lot of this.

He couldn't. "Okay. Tell me your idea."

She shook her head briskly. "No. You're right. Love of money is the root of all evil. Forget I mentioned anything. *Judge.* Maybe you can get a paper route."

"Goddamnit, Ellen, just tell me."

She set down her menu, looked into his eyes. "We get it from Art Lewis."

"Art Lewis? He's not parting with a nickel."

"I'm not saying we ask."

His mind suddenly experienced a peculiar vacancy. If you don't ask . . . what did he not understand?

"We *take*." She paused, stared into his soul. "We take what otherwise will be lost forever."

Conspiracy. Plain and simple, this was conspiracy. He'd sent bad men to prison for this. Exactly this.

"Lost when Art pops a tire fucking that slut. I've seen his will, Harry. All that money is going to bullshit. Libraries, colleges, UFOs, ESP."

"H-how do you know about the will?"

"A legal secretary at Kleinman Moscovitz."

He needed more to drink. "For Christ's sake, Ellen." The words came out as a parched whisper. "I'm a Superior Court judge." He waved his empty glass in the air.

She had him. "A judge is the first thing we need." She smiled brilliantly. "The second is a doctor. The third is a priest."

"A p-priest?"

"Of course, a priest, darling. When you can drag them off the altar boys."

CHAPTER SIX

What Latrell Said

"You know my mother?" Latrell had instantly read my fibissedah face. Like everyone did.

"Maybe I do." I looked into his eyes. If he was half as smart as his mother I'd be in trouble. "Okay, kid. You got two minutes. What's up?"

"I come 'bout my mom. She's in trouble."

"What kind of trouble?"

"People are comin' 'round. Telling her stuff. Bad stuff."

"What kind of people?"

"*Low* people." Latrell stared at me. "Low people. They don't want us livin' there no more. Say we gotta get out."

"Where do you live?"

"A Hundred Sixty-ninth and Hindemith."

"Bledsoe Park." Same place Nedra had lived back then. With her dad and brother. Reverend A. J. Scott and his fire-breathing son, Charles Scott, known nationally as Charles Ransom. Pay the ransom for the black man.

"They don't call it Bledsoe anymore."

"What do they call it?"

"It's what they *want* to call it. Azure Gardens."

"Nice name."

"They're gonna put in a lake."

"A *lake*?"

"They want to. They ain't gonna. 'Cause my mom ain't sellin'."

Latrell had five hundred dollars in cash.

"Where'd you get this?"

"Never mind where I got it. Here it is."

The start of any great journey is, of course, a single step. He pushed the money into my hand. My fingers closed around it. "I'm promising nothing. Your mother's going to have the last say, understand me?"

He nodded that he did.

"I'll come visit her."

"Thanks."

Now a little background. "Where'd you hear about me, Latrell?"

"Archie Deakins."

"Archie." I couldn't help smiling. "How's he doing?"

Latrell showed off his fade with a brush of his long, thin fingers. "He be cuttin' hair every day. And talkin' a mile a minute."

That was Archie. A font of wisdom, wit, and folklore. More commonly known as horseshit. One of the diamonds Archie had imparted to me: the mystery of the barber's phantom scissors.

Silk-clad Archie, weighing in at a stylish three-twenty, had come to me reluctantly. He had a barbershop in Lennox. In a strip mall. For fifteen years. But new people had come to call.

"Now I run a clean place, Mr. Dick, but its more than just a barbershop. *Everybody* come my place." He paused. "And I'm sure things go on that I don't know nothin' about." His eyebrows lifted. "Know what I mean?"

I could guess.

"So this man be threatenin' everybody. And everything. Through me, see? Gonna be talkin' I set 'em all up."

"He says he's a cop?"

"He say he got the man in his pocket."

"How do you know he's connected at all?"

"I don't. But he be threatenin'." He studied me again. "They say you the man."

"What does he want?"

"Thousand a month. For starters."

Blackmail. Plain and simple. "This man got anything solid on you?" In other words, do I negotiate.

"No. I run a clean operation. But like I said, everybody come my place."

In other words, things go down, but nothing too serious. "What do you want me to do?"

"I want you to kick his fuckin' ass down the street."

"Want me to kill him?"

Archie's mouth dropped open. Which was enough for me.

"No, no," said Archie, looking at me, the cure worse than the disease. "Maybe you the wrong man."

"I just had to check. I don't kill people."

He stared at me, distrustingly. "Whatcha gonna do?"

"I'll have a talk with the man. Your question is, how much does Dick Henry charge?"

"How much *do* Dick Henry charge?"

"That depends on what I have to do. But let's say five hundred up front, and we'll see."

Archie nodded, gauging me. Five hundred was bad news. But bad news he'd been expecting. "Okay, then."

"And one other thing."

"I knew it. I *knew* it. Always one other thing. And that's where the trouble be. What?"

"I know a kid who needs a job."

Archie, another fibissedah face, had practical concerns. "He gonna fit in 'round here?"

"He's black, Archie, if that's what you mean."

Archie showed me a wide expanse of teeth. In both gold and enamel. We'd been friends ever since.

CHAPTER SEVEN

Dennis Donnelly, Etta James

I was back in Venice again. But memories had been stirred up. Like a snow globe. These were streets I'd explored with Nedra.

Back then.

I rolled past the Peach Cat & Dog Hospital. No one out front. Good. Loman London was off pursuing easier economic opportunities. I made a left, then a right at Electric Avenue. I pulled over and parked.

I was looking at a purple house hung with a hundred mobiles and wind chimes.

Dennis Donnelly opened the door and I was ushered into a complete mess. An artist's mess. Pots of paint, canvases, rolls of tape, buckets of brushes, smoldering cigarettes. And somewhere a lost, lit joint. But then Dennis found it.

"Hey, Dick," he said, sucking in the good bud, "you know my old lady, right?"

I waved at Violet. She waved back. We knew each other. Hell, I know everybody. I'm the Shortcut Man.

"Hi, Dick," she said. She had long black curly hair, a bounteous chest, and, reaching her mid-thirties, a comfortable plumpness. "Can I roll you a fattie?"

"You can roll it for yourself."

"Good idea," said Dennis. "So what's up, Dick, my man?"

I found a vacant corner of the couch. "I have an interesting proposition for you."

"I'm ready for an interesting proposition," said Violet.

"She's ready for an interesting proposition," said Dennis, smiling.

Violet rolled a fattie with a flourish. A perfect cylinder.

I'd gone on the net and checked out Kostabi. Kind of a cool, detached, sci-fi vibe. Good color. "You know who Kostabi is?"

Dennis nodded. "Sure. Mark Kostabi. New York City dude. What about him?"

"Can you do a Kostabi?"

"You're talking about a painting."

"Yeah. A painting."

"He does music, too."

"Didn't know that."

"Of course Dennis can do Kostabi," said Violet, eye on the prize.

"Of course Dennis can," said Dennis, glancing at Violet with a smile. "She said so."

We laughed. "You know *Kostabi Number Five?*"

Dennis nodded. "I do know that painting. How much you offering?" The Oldsmobile's rear end had started fucking up. Violet wanted to drive to Portland for the Festival of the Roses.

"Four, five grand."

Violet looked at Dennis. "Well, uh, *five,* then."

"Yeah, five," said Dennis. Or should he have said six? Was there a catch here?

"Then five it is," I said.

"Five," said Violet.

"Five," repeated Dennis. He took another pull on the joint. Fuck it. A consensus had been reached. Seemingly.

I spread my hands. "Let's make it five, then."

There was a confused silence, then everybody laughed again. A venture had been launched. Everyone was happy.

"We're talking cash, right?" Dennis could see it all slipping away in contracts, promises, taxes, and IOUs. But then he remembered. This was Dick Henry. Dick Henry was the ultimo no-bullshit dude.

"Of course, cash."

"Well, we're in," said Violet. "And guess what?"

But my mind had turned to Nedra, to fortune cookies at Ah Fong's.

"Dick," said Violet, "you're distracted today."

"What?"

"You're distracted today."

"I am?"

"Yes, you are."

I shrugged. "Sorry."

"Guess who I saw yesterday?"

"I'm not a good guesser."

"I saw Puss. She'd want me to say hello."

Pussy Grace. Violet's sister on the pole. Christ Jesus. Now there was trouble. Pussy Grace. One thing after another, pillar to post. I mean pillar to pole. Trouble in endless variation with no end to it. "How is the old girl?"

Violet grinned. "Don't let her hear you say *old girl*."

Only a fool would do that. At the risk of physical remonstration.

"Because that would make me an old girl, too," concluded Violet, with frost.

"Oh, I didn't mean *physically*," I said, laying on the grease, grinning at Dennis. "Youth is a state of mind. You're nothing more than a foolish teenager."

Violet batted her eyes, allowed herself to be placated.

"So, how often you see Puss?"

"I go up to Hollywood once a week. For a singing lesson. With Mr. Montefiori."

"Singing lessons?"

"He's the best."

I left Dennis and Violet to their fattie, navigated Abbot Kinney to Pico. There I banged a left, the towers of downtown Los Angeles ahead in the haze.

Fortune cookies. We'd taken them, mixed them up, so fate would truly have its way, then opened them and read.

Dance as if no one is watching. That was mine.

The one you love is closer than you think. That was hers.

"Let's dance," I said, offering my hand across the table.

"Okay," she replied, dark eyes wide and serious.

Ah Fong's was an eatery, not a place for dancing. It didn't matter. I still recall the pressure of her fingers as she took my hand. Nedra was looking at me with the same expression I think I was wearing. Things were so perfect, yet so delicate. Like it was foreordained.

We came together in the narrow aisle that divided the ten little tables right and left. Ray Charles finished up and Etta James dropped down to take his place. *At Last.*

I put my right hand on her hip and she moved into me.

We danced.

I still can remember every second. If I want to. The thud of my heart in my throat. The grit under my shoes. The best three minutes of my life. And I knew it, felt it as it ran out, second by second.

The future had opened up before me, virgin, unlimited, unparalleled, untrammeled. Where mist and cloud had occluded my vision I now saw with diamond clarity. The universe was ancient and welcoming. I had purpose and mission and inspiration.

And here we are in heaven. For you are mine at last.

CHAPTER EIGHT

Vices and Spices

The Cherokee Hotel wasn't shit as far as trendy addresses went, and it wasn't shit anyway. A working girl courting a wrecking ball. Some dopeheads, some whores, a few dealers, some speed-freak musicians, that asshole with the wandering eye trying to write the great American novel. Some writers would buy squalor. Felt obliged to buy it.

No, the Cherokee wasn't anybody's final destination. It was a place you hung, precariously, for the moment, until you fell off or rescued yourself.

Mr. Bobby Lebow didn't give a shit. He'd seen better. Much better. He'd had automobiles, he'd had houses, he'd had a small plane, he'd had a fucking yacht, he'd had a record contract, he'd had plans. Had a retinue of hangers-on, both professional and amateur.

Now all of that was long gone. But, at this moment, he was happy. Not Jesus-personal-savior happy, but all the same. In a drawer below the surface of his coffee table, in his totally trashed, fucked-up hole of an apartment, was a plastic bag with almost an ounce of cocaine in it.

Yes, he was happy. The front door was locked, he had his Brillo pads, he had his pipes, he had his Bics, he had his vials, he had his baking soda, he had his pocketknife, he had his paper towels, and on that little mirror was a two-gram pile of cocaine. And with what was in the drawer, *yes, it was still there,* twenty-six delicious grams, he could maintain the mellow wire for four or five days. Before he had to scuttle over the hills into the Valley and score another piece.

Even though he was anxious for that first hit, he allowed himself the discomfort of anticipation, as he surveyed his resources. Yes. Oh, *yes.* Everything was in order.

But then, what was that he saw on the rug? Right between his feet? He picked it up; joy surged through him. Big as a pencil eraser, irregular as a Martian moon, a good four-hit rock of crack cocaine was couched between thumb and forefinger.

He set it down on the Miles Davis CD, *In a Silent Way,* that had temporarily become the center of all things. He broke a chunk off, put it in the tube end of the liquor spout that he used, with the copper Brillo as a filter, as his crack pipe. He picked up a little red Bic. It worked. Then he brought flame to the end of the spout.

Listening hard, as the fragrant purple-tasting pebble gave up its magic in that wonderful stream of tiny crepitations, he drew the cocaine vapor deep into his lungs. Before he set the pipe down, the cocaine had crossed his blood-brain barrier and he was off.

Oh, yeah. It was good to be Bobby Lebow.

In her yellow 1988 Mercedes SL 450 hardtop with tinted windows, Ellen Havertine passed Musso & Frank's, made a left at Cherokee, parked in the lot behind Hollywood's oldest restaurant. One of the three Hispanics crammed into the parking kiosk gave her a ticket, not giving her a second glance. Probably couldn't read. Grew up in a mud hut.

She walked down the steps into Musso's, turned right, heading for the dining room, but stopped at the old wooden phone booths. Fifty cents later she had her ex-husband on the line.

"Come on over," said Bobby.

* * *

The Cherokee was a fucking dump. But the people she needed to see didn't live at the Four Seasons. She climbed to the third floor, delicately walked to the end of the hall. Who knew what loathsome things lived in that carpet. A long time ago, it may have been yellow. Bad choice. It would probably ruin her shoes. She knocked at 3G.

She heard Bobby moving around and then the door opened.

"Well, well, well," said Bobby, "the judge's wife."

He pointed to a chair across the coffee table. The chair was filled with papers, magazines, and pizza boxes. "Just push that shit onto the floor."

She looked at him questioningly.

"Just push that shit onto the floor. That's the way I like it."

So she did. And sat down carefully. She hadn't seen Bobby in how long? A couple of years. He'd gone downhill. He was thinner. "Where's what's-his-name? Didn't you used to have a dog?"

"Used to."

"What happened to him?"

"He took a shit in the kitchen." Bobby volunteered nothing further.

"And? Then what?"

"Then he had to fuckin' go, that's what. He started walkin' funny."

"Intestinal problems?"

"No. I kicked him in the head. And he blew a fuse. So he had to go. You here for animal rights or something?"

"No."

"Then mind your own business. You know the last thing to go through a parakeet's mind when you throw him against the wall?"

"Don't be gruesome."

"His ass. Now howya been?"

"Fine, Bobby. How about you?"

"Same ol', same ol', same ol'. I'm just about to cook up a couple grams. Want a hit?"

Half of her mind instantly dissolved into a chemical longing. You never forgot. No matter how long it had been. "No," she said.

"Suit yourself." She wouldn't last.

With a playing card, the Jack of Hearts, he dug into the pile of cocaine and transferred half of it into the vial. He added a thumbnail of baking soda and water, shook it up.

Ellen had been watching like a hawk. "I'll have one hit."

Bobby laughed. "That's more like it."

"Just one."

He brought a Bic to the bottom of the vial, which he shook in a circle, applying the necessary heat to turn cocaine and baking soda into crack. "You bring my money, bitch?"

"Don't talk to me that way, Bobby. Even if you're joking."

"I'm not joking. You got my money?"

"It's in the mail, as always." She'd almost forgotten his belligerent rudeness.

"It'd better be."

In the vial, sludgy, thick boogers of crack had formed. He stopped swirling and they sank gently to the bottom. Bobby held it up to the light. *Bingo,* all systems go. He wiped the soot off the bottom of the vial, satisfied.

He poured the water in the vial through a paper towel into the trash can. Then the soft rocks were tumbled onto the CD. He sectioned them up with his pocketknife and troweled some of the sludge into the ends of two liquor-spout pipes.

He slid one across to Ellen, followed by a Bic. Bitch could hardly wait. "Bon appetit, baby."

He picked up his pipe, watched her go, delaying his own pleasure.

She heard that faint crackling that heralded paradise. And then she was off. *Ohhh, Ellen. Goooooood God.*

Bobby watched the cocaine ring the big bell in her pleasure center. Right now he could stand up, go over there, stuff her face with cock and she'd take it. But been there done that. It wasn't worth the trouble.

He rang his own bell. Absolutely loved the taste. A taste you never forgot. The taste you dreamed of when it was all gone. When you were desperately scraping out old pipes and searching the carpet for shards.

A wave of well-being rolled through him. Shit in hand, *in hand,* he was on the first steps of a five-day yellow brick road. Dreams and plans would rise to meet the clear surety of execution. It was good to be Bobby Lebow.

"So, tell me the scheme."

"You're sworn to secrecy."

"*Secrecy?* Doesn't Superior Court Judge Harry Glidden's wife have her cum-soaked lips wrapped around a crack pipe at this very moment? How much secrecy do you need?"

The second toke floated in, rang her gong again. *Float like a butterfly, sting like a goddamn bee.* She sat back.

"So tell me the plan," said Bobby. "Just the hints you've given me. You're fuckin' broke."

"We're not broke. Our circumstances are a little straightened."

Hilarious. "You didn't marry the lame lawman for straightened circumstances."

"Regardless, Bobby. It's Art Lewis we're worrying about."

"I've heard of him . . . I think. Art Lewis—the unscrupulous developer."

"Every developer's unscrupulous. Or you don't make money. Art made his first fortune selling screws to the Chinese."

"Almost as good as the rice business."

"I'd rather be in the bowl business."

"But Mr. Unscrupulous doesn't want to lend you anything."

"We offered him a sure thing."

"Another one of those filthy rich fools."

She took a clean-up hit off the smoked pipe. A muted bell sounded. "Art is seventy-five. We know him socially. He loves banging sluts. But his current one is going to kill him."

"She looks good, eh?"

"She's pretty. Nice ass, nice tits. Ex–pole dancer."

Bobby grinned. "What's not to love, baby?"

"The trouble is, when he pops a gasket, all his money is going to ESP research, reincarnation, UFO stupidities. And other bullshit."

"That would be a goddamn shame."

"Yes, it would."

"So, what are you going to do?"

She slid her pipe across for a refill. "We're going to marry him off. And then when he goes, the estate will be divided appropriately."

"Won't the wife get everything?"

"His wife will be our hired gun."

"Too bad *you* can't marry him. You got class. But you married that penniless blowhard instead."

"The hard part is the marriage itself."

"Isn't it always? Why would Art Lewis get married? That's the last thing on his mind. When you're bored with a slut you rent another. So what are you going to do?"

"He lives out in Temescal. We're going to get out there and administer the proper chemicals."

"In his own house."

"Yes."

"*Aha.* And in that state he's going to get married."

"Exactly."

"Who performs the ceremony?"

"Ceremony? All we need is paper."

"Harry's in on this?"

"Yes."

"Righteous." Got to hand it to the bitch. This was an idea worth having. "Who's he gonna marry? Eileen?"

"Eileen is as stupid as a goat. We need someone with class, like you said. I'm thinking Erin Halle."

He flicked his Bic, rode the new wave. "Erin Halle. In principle, I agree. But isn't she in a lot of trouble?"

"Without help, Erin Halle is going to jail."

He grinned. "Here comes Uncle Harry. You've thought of everything."

"I just need a drug regimen."

"My specialty."

"Your specialty."

He put his hands behind his head and thought. "First, you soften him up. Rohypnol. Second, you flatten him out, Placidyl with Fentanyl back. Third, you keep him off balance with an antipsychotic like clozapine or Haldol. Or better yet, Prolixin if we can still find it." He took a second hit off his pipe. "I can get them all. Except maybe Prolixin."

"What's Prolixin?"

"What fucked Gary Gilmore. In prison."

He reached for her pipe, refilled both of them. "When does this all go down?"

"Soon as we can."

CHAPTER NINE

A Library Stinker

The sun was shining as I drifted down Santa Monica Boulevard, heading east, past the morning prostitutes, past the morning transvestite prostitutes, past the little theater district, past Cole Field, where I'd played ball as a kid. Hey, batta batta.

I'd gotten a call fifteen minutes ago from Mrs. Dunlap. How in hell had she gotten my number? Didn't matter. Probably through Jack.

Mrs. Dunlap had been my fifth-grade teacher when I was called Richard and had been considered a student with possibilities. She had gone on to a second career as a librarian for the city of Los Angeles. I had gone on to become the Shortcut Man. Now she was the system's oldest employee, still sharp as a tack, apparently.

She held down the fort at the Cahuenga Library, a forlorn outpost of civilization near the corner of Santa Monica and Vermont. With diminishing funds, in a neighborhood where few people visited the library anymore, and even fewer spoke English, Mrs. Dunlap soldiered on.

On the phone she'd been insistent but so polite I wasn't sure what she was talking about. I walked up the broad stone steps and entered.

In an instant I knew what Mrs. Dunlap's problem was. All the windows were wide open. With nary a customer but one.

A large, shabby man was at a reading table, head down, dozing. There, in all his reeking, solitary disglory, was a library stinker. The stench of long unwashed human flesh was beyond horrible and emanated in waves from the miscreant. I tried not to breathe through my nose.

Mrs. Dunlap approached. She wasn't breathing either.

"Thank you for coming, Richard."

I nodded painfully. "You got a stinker, eh?"

"Well, he's not doing much reading."

"But he's doing a whole lot of stinking."

Mrs. Dunlap gathered her sweater more tightly about her shoulders. With age, fresh air had a price.

"I called the police, Richard."

"Yeah?" They wouldn't do a goddamn thing.

"They said he was within his rights."

Of course. *Within his rights.* What about the rights of the kids, the old people, the regular folks who appreciated a tiny oasis of learning and relaxation in the vast, trashy, depressing, sullen monstrosity that was Los Angeles?

I looked around for the exits. "Where's the back door around here, Mrs. Dunlap?"

She pointed across the room.

Okay. I knew what I had to do. "Close the library for a minute, Mrs. Dunlap. Like you do at night."

This went against protocol. "Oh, I'm not allowed to do that, Richard."

But it had to be done. I pulled a flashy health club card from my wallet. It was a holographic specimen of many colors.

I waved it in front of her. I didn't belong to the club but what the hell. "Go ahead. It's alright. Close up."

"Ohhh. Alright, Richard."

"Then take a short walk. Go across the street and get a Coke."

"I don't drink Coke, Richard."

No matter what you did in this world, there were right ways and wrong ways. "Then why don't you get a little air. You could use it. *I* could use it. I'm going to have a man-to-man with the stinker."

"You're not going to hurt him, are you, Richard?"

My God. This was truly a fine woman, and a pacifist to boot. If only I had been born in 1930. But I wouldn't have measured up. "Are you a Buddhist, Mrs. Dunlap?"

"No, I'm a Christian Scientist. But I respect all faiths."

"As do I. Don't worry." I walked her to the door, sent her out.

The stinker had his head up. I walked over.

"Hey, buddy." Good God, I wanted to puke. "What's your name?"

"What's it to you?"

"It's for the office."

"What office?"

"The coroner's office."

"Uhhh, the coroner's off—whaddaya mean?"

"I mean they'll be calling the coroner's office after I'm done with you. After I rip off your head and shit down your neck. Now, what's your name?"

"Rutland Atwater."

"Rutland Atwater. Well, Rutland, I need you to go someplace else."

"And where would you suggest I go?"

A smart-ass as well. "The possibilities are infinite. But the choice is yours."

"Fine. I think I'll stay here. The police have already been here. They say I'm within my rights."

Assholes and their rights. I was filled with a sudden rage. I walked over, knelt down, and yanked the chair out from under him.

Atwater landed on the floor like a heavy sack of fertilizer, fomenting an updraft of stomach-turning air.

48

Rising, steeling myself, I grabbed him by the back of the collar and dragged him toward the rear exit.

"Hey! I know the law! You're making a big mistake!"

I hit the exit bar with my back, the door opened, and then we were in the parking lot.

I hated to think what was on my hands. I saw a spigot and rinsed and rinsed and rinsed.

Then I went over to asshole. "Listen to me. Don't ever, ever, ever go back into that library again. Got me?"

The stinker, sitting on the pavement, hands propped behind him, nodded. "I don't have any olfactory glands," he bleated.

"I don't give a fuck about your glands, Stanley."

"Rutland," corrected the stinker meekly.

I'd used Stanley generically. An idea struck me. "You know the old lady who works here?"

"What about her?"

"See. You're not so smart."

"What about her?"

"You say you know the law?"

"Loyola School of Law."

"Loyola? Then you must know what happens to old ladies who commit terrible crimes."

"Uhhh, no. What happens?"

"Nothing happens, you stupid son of a bitch. Nothing happens. I just saved your ass, see? She was going to set you on fire."

"*Fire?*"

"Fire. Don't test her. She's my grandmother. On my mother's side. She looks sweet as pie but all her tacos aren't on one plate. She was the one who burned down the Pan-Pacific Auditorium in 1989." Or whatever year it had burned down.

"No shit."

"Yeah. Yeah. You owe me, Rutland." Christ. Now I knew this

misfit's name. Because it had penetrated my consciousness at an angle; because I had made no effort to remember it.

"The Pan-Pacific? Jesus. I didn't know."

"Jesus had nothing to do with it."

And that's how the Shortcut Man restored order and tranquillity to the last bastion of civilization on east Santa Monica Boulevard.

Now the day's real trial was ahead. At one o'clock I was visiting Nedra Scott.

CHAPTER TEN

Nedra Scott

Bledsoe Park had quickened in the '40s to house the black population migrating west for the wartime jobs downtown. Fifty-some years later, when I had come to visit Nedra, the neighborhood looked its age, for the most part battered but still proud, here and there someone holding out to the last man, the house and yard pristine. White picket fence, palm tree, weathervane. The Right Reverend Asa J. Scott had one such house.

Twenty years after my last visit, I pushed through a ring of liquor stores and fast-food places into a dilapidated war zone.

At at stop sign by a school, a streetlamp arched high. It took me a few seconds to realize that every square inch of the streetlamp had been grafittied. *Every square inch.* Even way up where you'd think no one could possibly get to.

To me it was a clear sign. The battle of Bledsoe Park had been convincingly and completely lost.

It reminded me of a young lieutenant's Vietnam War chronicle. The Americans had taken a village, had inoculated the children against whatever threats American children were inoculated against. Later, in the tide of war, the village had been lost. Then it had been recovered. The soldiers reentered, only to meet a large group of one-armed children. The Cong had hacked off the arms of all inoculated children.

The lieutenant realized in that moment the war was lost. His soldiers, as professional and well trained as they were, possessed no singleness of purpose like the Cong. It was just a matter of time. And blood.

I rolled to the next stop sign. Its streetlight was also fully grafittied. No hope for Bledsoe Park. Bring on Azure Gardens.

Nedra's house was exactly as it had been. Neat and clean. But the surrounding houses stood raggedly, in grim fatigue against gravity. My shiny white Cadillac looked like a conveyance from another solar system.

I knocked and waited. Then the door was pulled back.

Nedra had aged. Still beautiful. Harder. Her eyes were not defeated, but they were tired. "Come in, Dick, come in."

She led me to the kitchen. "Coffee?"

"Yes, please." I watched her at work. Grinding some beans, filling the filter, measuring and pouring some water. For a second I felt I could reach and touch her, that I could erase all that had come between us.

"Cream?"

"As always," I said, bringing the past forward.

She placed two heavy cups on the table. Through the worn-out photo glaze I recognized them from the Grand Central Market. Where we had luxuriated in our secrets. She sat down.

We looked at one another. A gray kitten wandered through the kitchen, under her chair. It peered up at me. It had one eye. She saw me look.

"That's Wide-Track."

My expression must have been interrogatory.

"Wide-Track Pontiac," she continued. "He's got six toes every-where. And he's got one eye, but around here we roll with the upside."

"I had a one-eyed cat, too."

"And you called him—?"

"Hi-Beam."

She smiled. "That sounds like you, Dick." She took a sip of her coffee and we set in. "So Latrell paid you a visit."

"Yes. Found his way to Hollywood. On your behalf. He thinks you're in trouble of some kind."

"When am I not in trouble of some kind?"

"He told me a little about Azure Gardens."

"And a little is all you need to know, Dick. Some white people from downtown are looking for some cheap real estate and they've decided Bledsoe Park is the place. Nothing better for real estate prices than to get rid of the *black people* who live here. Who've lived here for seventy years."

She went on. I started having an odd feeling. That I was listening to something preprepared. Not directed at me in particular. "Are people threatening you, Nedra?"

"Yes, fucking people are threatening me."

"Can I help?"

"I don't need your help, Dick." She got up, opened a drawer, pulled out a .38-caliber revolver, held it up. "If there's trouble, I say, *bring it on.*"

Her voice was pained and harsh, her face stone.

We hung there for a second. Then she lowered the gun, put it back in the drawer. "Sorry."

"I think you *do* need a little help here. The average woman in this town doesn't have a gun right at hand, ready to use."

"I'm not the average woman, am I, Dick?"

"No, you're not."

"As long as we understand that. So I'll do things my way, thank you very much."

Sun Tzu and his *Art of War* floated into my mind. *Some battles are not meant to be fought.* Part of the Shortcut canon. "Can I be honest?"

"Nothing's ever stopped you before."

Point to Nedra.

"And I mean no disrespect in what I'm going to say."

"Just speak your mind, Dick."

"My question is this: I drove here through a war zone. The battle of Bledsoe Park is lost. The forces of anarchy have won, hands down. Why are you here? Why the hell are you still here?"

She stared at me with dangerous, glittering eyes. "Only this black woman knows her connection to her land, Dick. I won't be moved. By a bunch of downtown rabbits. Now, did my son mention any other problems?"

"Yes, he did." I knew this next part wasn't going to go over well. "He wants to know what happened to Uncle Charles."

That required some reflection. "He would come to you for *that*?"

"Well, he did."

Nedra shook her head. She smiled but there was no light in it. "Don't we all know what happened to my brother? I do. You do. Everyone around here knows. And the United States government knows."

"I guess Latrell is naive."

"Of course Latrell is naive. He lives with his mother, who protects him." She looked at me, thinking, other responses being considered. But she opted out. "Thanks for stopping by, Dick," she said. "Why don't you go home now?"

I slipped in some Pearly King, rolled for Hollywood. Pearly and the Temple Thieves had done a nice cover of a Little Walter tune, "Still

Your Fool." My vintage Cadillac tube radio gave it that luscious, fat sound.

Charles Scott, Latrell's uncle, had been a very difficult thorn in local politics, then, briefly, in national politics. Then he disappeared into thin air. Vanished. Nothing was proven, one way or another.

Which proved everything.

CHAPTER ELEVEN

A Proposal of Marriage

Erin Halle's place was around here somewhere. A million years ago Ellen had been to a party there and met Erin, kissed air. This was the unknown section of Hollywood Boulevard, where it wandered into the hills above Crescent Heights, a curving two-lane shadow of itself.

She parked the yellow Mercedes. The place had gone to seed. Literally and figuratively. A gardener was of very secondary importance when one nurtured an appetite for cocaine.

She rang the bell and waited. Erin would probably be fifty. It had been at least twenty years since the television show *Houston* had been a primetime spectacle. Fifty meant choosing either one's face or one's body.

The skeleton who opened the door had chosen neither. She had chosen cocaine. Nervous eyes played over the visitor. "Do I know you?"

"We've met but you may not remember me."

"Why are you here?"

"Because I have your get-out-of-jail-free card."

"Come in."

The breakfast nook had a nice view of West Los Angeles below.

Erin Halle sat facing away from that view, looking down on her cocaine paraphernalia. Unapologetically, she packed the end of a long glass tube, flicked her Bic.

Now she was ready to talk. "What was your name, again?"

"Ellen."

"Ellen. Can I fix you a hit, Ellen?"

"Not my thing," said Ellen.

"Good." Erin nodded. She flicked her Bic, exhaled. "Why are you here?"

"Because I need your services."

"Nobody needs me anymore."

"I do."

"Explain."

"First let me say, I'm an actress, too, and that I always thought you were very good. Very, very good." Well, good. Pretty good.

"Thank you." Erin searched her memory. But her memory wasn't associating all that well this year. Who was this woman? She did look familiar. Then the woman's name fell into her head. Ellen. *Ellen Havertine.* "You're Ellen Havertine."

"That's me."

"We've worked together!"

"Yes, we have."

"What did we do?"

"I guested on *Houston* a few times, then we did a Ronald Reagan biopic thing. And probably some other stuff, too."

"As long as we got paid."

"We did. Look, Erin. I also know you're in trouble. That you might go to jail."

Erin lit up, exhaled. "That's what they say."

"I can help."

"How can you help?"

"I can get you off."

Erin shook her head quickly, birdlike. "No one can do that. It's an open-and-shut case. I'm screwed."

Ellen showed her hand. "If you marry the man I'm going to suggest to you, I can make sure you don't go to jail."

"*Marry?* Me marry?"

"Marry. Then you'll share your new husband's assets with me."

If that wasn't an excuse to take a hit, nothing was. She took one. Two. She looked up at the lady. Things fell into place. This woman was on that piece-of-crap cable show *Special Counsel.* She *was* the Special Counsel! Things got curiouser and curiouser. "So let me get this straight. You're going to fix my case and I'm going to marry Mr. X." This was audacious enough to actually work. Because what often succeeded in life *was* audacity.

"That's the plan."

"Guarantee me I'll get off?"

"You won't go to jail."

"And, then, after I get married, I'll be turning Mr. X's assets over to you."

"Most of them. But there'll be something substantial in there for you, don't worry."

This was like a bad TV movie. Out of the blue came the perfect solution. A delirious joy filled her. Better take a hit. So she did. A soft red rose of emotion materialized in her heart. "Is my husband a nice man?"

CHAPTER TWELVE

Art and Justice

Judge Glidden's courtroom was on the seventh floor of the House of Justice on Temple Street. I'd parked within sight of Gehry's Disney Hall and walked over.

Professional day-to-day justice was a dismal thing. Old suits, old briefcases, old shoes, old strategies, old jokes. The only thing new was today's defendant. Who looked just like yesterday's defendant. Who often *was* yesterday's defendant.

But today I was there for a different purpose. My purpose was art. Kostabi.

A matter was in progress and I took a seat in the back. The courtroom was nearly deserted except for the concerned.

"The defendant will approach the bench." The bailiff, a large, forbidding black man, had seen it all.

The defendant looked familiar. I wondered what she'd done. Good God, she'd been beautiful. And still was. No doubt she'd had to kick a path through the broken hearts at her doorstep. Now she was skinny, actually very skinny, but dressed well and made up well.

Then I recognized her. Erin something. Erin *Halle.* One of the stars of *Houston.* She'd been Pamela Lorrilard, Texas aristocrat, a wealthy bitch who'd supported the opera and the museum but killed people for demanding a share of the water that flowed across her land. A civic-minded dame.

She stood beside her lawyer.

I recognized him, too. Andy Rigrod. A very sharp character. Rigrod, famously, could manufacture reasonable doubt out of mist and whole cloth.

Glidden opened his mouth and out came that TV baritone. He hadn't been using it at the Pantry. "Miss Halle, you've pleaded guilty to the possession of three-point-two-three ounces of crack cocaine. Is that right?"

She looked at Rigrod. He nodded.

"Yes, Your Honor," she said.

"And cocaine paraphernalia. Is that right?"

Rigrod nodded again.

"Yes, Your Honor."

"Ms. Halle, I've read your support documents from your friends, family, fans, and physicians. And I have some sympathy for your addictions, which you state as both to cocaine and to alcohol. But I assume you do know right from wrong. Am I correct?"

With the added authority of position, Glidden spoke with great heaviness.

Ms. Halle swallowed. "Yes, Your Honor."

"Ms. Halle, your crime is punishable by no less than ten years in state prison and no more than sixteen years in state prison. Because this matter involves rock cocaine, not powder cocaine, there are sentencing guidelines. In accordance with these guidelines, I hereby sentence you to ten years in state prison."

Ms. Halle cried out and bent at the waist. Her voice echoed around the drabness. Then there was just the sound of her sobs, dry and pitiful. Rigrod reached out, grabbed her arm.

Whew. Even if someone caused their own train wreck this moment was difficult to watch. The reckoning.

"But," Glidden continued, "because I believe you are truly contrite, and this is your first major offense in a long life of hard work, with many documented charitable works, I'm going to set the guidelines aside. I'm suspending the sentence to time served with the remainder to be served on probation."

Ms. Halle gasped, unsure of what she'd just heard.

"In addition, I'm mandating a rehabilitation program, at least twenty-six weeks in duration, outpatient. One more thing, Ms. Halle. If you're found with as much as one single nonprescription Percocet, Valium, Vicodin, Oxycontin, anything—you're going to prison. For a long time. Is that clear?"

"Yes, Your Honor." Her voice a ghostly whisper.

The gavel slammed down and the lady fell into the arms of Rigrod.

Ten minutes later I was ushered into Glidden's private office by the bailiff. The judge, still in his black robes, was behind his desk.

"Was I too lenient, Mr. Henry? The prosecutors seemed to think so."

I shrugged. The waters of justice ran deep. "You must have your reasons, Judge."

"And I do." He gestured me into a seat.

I sat.

He looked at me with his famous hawklike expression. "So. What's up, Mr. Henry?"

"Well, I've found your man. Ten thousand dollars."

"That's just what you estimated."

"It so happens."

He nodded. "I'll give you eight."

No way I was going to drive all the way to Venice for three grand. "You'll give me twelve."

Glidden laughed. "Okay, ten. But I had to try."

"Of course." I wasn't the only game in town, but the other players lurked in the dark. Generally, it was always best to lurk in the dark. If you had to lurk at all. "Do you have the work in question, Judge?"

He pointed over to the couch. A large green paper shopping bag. I went over, pulled it out.

Right off, from what I saw on the Internet, I loved Kostabi. But standing in front of the actual painting was a big step up.

Kostabi #5 was the depiction of a squarish perfume bottle. In or on the bottle were two lovers with featureless faces, mannequinlike, in a tender embrace.

"Isn't it wonderful?" said the judge. He was reverent, searching my face.

What's art? I don't know. I just know what I like. The Temple Thieves had weighed in on the subject in their song "Devotion":

> *Art is the sum of what is not*
> *in all the books*
> *ain't no school teach between the lines*
> *love is the hope this ain't no joke*
> *we're all bleedin' through*
> *I thank God every day that I am blind*
> *and other days I cannot see*

I nodded at Judge Glidden. "I like it. And I'll get you a good copy."

"It has to almost fool me."

"That might be hard to do." Anyone with teeth that white was susceptible to flattery.

"It *will* be hard to do."

"I'll get it done."

"Who's going to do it?"

"With all due respect, Your Honor, that's none of your business." Like what people think of the Shortcut Man. *None of my business.*

Hangin' Harry nodded his head.

CHAPTER THIRTEEN

Pussy Grace

If Kiyoko had been more reasonable I would never have accepted Pussy Grace's invitation. But Kiyoko currently considered me a barbarian and considered all attempts at reconciliation acts of disrespect. Which was pretty shortsighted of her. Me being a prince and all.

Most of our squabbles were based on misunderstandings of English, word or idiom. But pointing this out pissed her off.

Are you saying I can't speak English?

That's not what I'm saying.

I speak English all over the world.

I have no doubt you have.

Then she dropped the Big Conclusion and I realized I could never win:

Every time we argue you say I can't speak English.

Meaning that I spitefully attacked her delivery to avoid the point of what she was saying.

No, dearest. You have it backwards. We argue because concepts escape you—because you don't understand English as well as you might if you'd been born in California. Where Dick Henry, your dim, monolinguistic friend was born. *Forku. Porku.*

So I found myself driving through the guitar district of Hollywood looking for Puss's place.

The guitar district itself was testament that the most important concept in the retail music business was mediocrity.

All of us possessed an Inner Star. The trouble was bringing him or her out. A burning talent required just an acoustic guitar and an audience. Bob Dylan. A less talented Inner Star might require a shiny new red electric guitar with two necks, a huge amp, a fuzz pedal, a chorus pedal, an echo pedal, a studded belt, a spiky haircut, some suede boots, an eyebrow piercing, another guitar or two, and a few more amps. Then, twenty thousand dollars later, he was almost prepared to get ready to get started to commence to begin. Planned for the morrow, of course.

After Gardner Street was Sierra Bonita, where Puss lived. Her house was a white, sturdily built Hollywood bungalow. She opened up the door and was apparently overjoyed to see me. She crushed her boobs against my chest. And, of course, regardless of whose boobs, and how they came to be, that part of a feminine greeting always did feel pretty good.

I'd met Puss after the unscheduled delivery of a pumpkin pie. *That* pumpkin pie. When I was no longer welcome in my own home, she welcomed me into her life, nonexclusively, and allowed me to put my cares and woes aside for a moment or two.

On the negative side, she was a catalyst for trouble, bringing it down on others, remaining blithely untouched herself.

You're acting as her chauffeur, because she's too high to drive. You're driving around town like a gleeful maniac in the reddest, most powerful Dodge Viper on the planet.

You congratulate her on her good fortune. You ask her when she acquired this amazing vehicle.

This morning, she says with a giggle.

This *morning*?

The keys were on my kitchen table.

What do you mean?

I mean the keys were on my kitchen table.

Slowly, her words sink in. This car—it isn't yours?

No. Is that a problem?

It sure the fuck is a problem. You open the glove box. *Great.* There's a gun. And a big bag of white powder. Then you hear the thudding noise. From the trunk. *In* the trunk.

Puss isn't worried. Let's grab a burger.

Luckily, beneath the stoplight at Sweetzer and Sunset, I pull up next to Bosto Ket, the mellifluous, phony Nigerian with a minor in shortcut work.

Dick, my good man. What the fuck are you doing in Q-Pain's automobile?

Who's Q-Pain?

Compton's angriest rapper. Especially now.

Why now?

His car's been stolen.

Puss was as beautiful as she'd ever been. Which always made visiting Pussy a risk. This time, however, I swore to uphold my virtue and not allow myself to be dragged into another of her reckless escapades.

I was reaffirming that vow an hour later when I saw her bottle of Two-Buck Chuck was three-quarters down.

"More wine, Dick?"

I waved her off and cautioned her. "You drink any more of that, you'll be forgetting your promise and sitting on my lap."

Pussy giggled.

I should have run. But I didn't.

If only Kiyoko had called. But she didn't.

Next thing I knew we were in bed. Her body was outrageous and she knew it. She knew how to tease and took great pleasure in it. From practice with each other, we made good, long love.

She achieved the clouds and rain, once, twice, thrice. Then, eyes half-closed with sated lust, she asked me one of my favorite questions. "Where do you want to come, Dick?"

I told her and she made it happen.

It was good. Very good. I was about to say that we should do this more often when the more mature part of me remembered doing this more often would only lead to the same stuff it led to before. So I asked her a different question.

"Why am I here, Puss?" Her distressed call, last night, had interrupted a frustrating game of mau-mau with Rojas. I had just played my last card, winning, but had neglected, in conclusion, to say "this is a game called mau-mau." With that omission, I carefully snatched defeat from the jaws of victory, sending Rojas into an fit of table-pounding laughter.

"Dude," he spluttered, delighted, "you be playin' like a white man." Whatever that meant.

Puss was lost in her thoughts. I had to ask my question again. "*Puss. Why am I here?*"

She laughed a satisfied laugh. "To scratch my back, hon. Just like old times."

"That's the wine talking."

She raised a finger. "No. That's the wine singing."

She lit a cigarette with my Zippo. "You're here because I need you. You know I've been dating Art Lewis, right?"

I shrugged. "Should I know who that is?"

"The real estate developer."

Apparently everyone else in the world knew who he was. Fine. "Maybe I have heard of him. Nice guy?"

"Yes. And we have a good thing happening. We're not going to be married or anything, but—but we've got a thing."

"Congratulations." Maybe she needed a Sunday Man. Another tune by Pearly. "So, what's happening with him?"

"That's the thing. I haven't been able to get in touch with him. For a week. More than a week, actually. Ten days. He's never not called me for this long before."

"So what?" Maybe the nonmessage was a message in itself.

"And different people answer the phone."

"So you leave messages."

"I've left twenty messages. Everyone's unfriendly."

"Unfriendly how?"

"Like they don't know me and Art. You know, as a couple."

What could I say? It didn't seem to add up to all that much. "I don't know Art well enough to judge this. Nothing is waving a flag, here. For me."

"Well, I see a flag."

"Okay. Is that all? Is there anything else?"

"There is something else." Pussy smiled and I knew I'd screwed up. "Scratch my back again, Dick."

I gathered my strength. "No."

She shrugged. "Suit yourself." Then she rolled over on her stomach, pushed her ass up. Her perfect ass. She looked over her shoulder and wiggled. "Look, Dick, look."

Run, Dick, run.

But I didn't.

CHAPTER FOURTEEN

Goodbye to All That

Although Puss had her twisted way with me, at least I woke up in my own bed. After a coffee I called Bosto Ket. I'd asked him to keep an eye out for Nedra down in the war zone and he'd said he would.

"Just some young African-American freelancers down there, Dick. Working for some lowlife at Azure Gardens, LLC. Out of one of them construction-site trailer offices. A verbal contract. They were gonna get a fee for getting Ms. Scott to move on. They didn't know who she was exactly."

"You explained?"

"I had my long gun to one of the fucker's ears. He was listenin.' Hard."

I smiled. Education was expensive.

Bosto went on. "At first, they thought they *might* have heard of Brother Charles. In a little bit they were sure that they had. Then they found out Nedra Scott was his sister. That's when the shit start to move. They didn't know she was *that* Ms. Scott. I told 'em no Ms. Scott would be dissed on my planet. Then I pulled the trigger. *Click.*" Bosto laughed. "And then I do believe I smelled shit."

As I ate the Egg King's breakfast I saw Nedra's face on TV and turned it up. Bosto had indeed done his work. She was alive and kicking.

She was being interviewed in front of her house by Ted Sargent, a square-jawed, empty moron who blabbed for Channel 9 and was out of his depth with Nedra Scott. Conveniently irate at the Bledsoe injustice, he appeared afraid of Nedra and the neighborhood in general, his eyes darting right and left.

Nedra radiated a cold anger and spoke precisely in the King's English. "It comes down to this, ladies and gentlemen. Black people will not be pushed out of Bledsoe Park. Our blood, sweat, and tears are in the soil here. My father's blood, sweat, and tears. I will not sell my home. The downtown, moneyed, white interests will not put up Azure Park on our land. On my land. *It's not going to happen.*"

"Look around," she commanded with a sweep of her arm. The cameras panned over the wreckage: abandoned houses, junked cars, accreted garbage. A medley of wrack and ruin. "The downtown *white* interests *let this happen.* And now that it looks like *they planned it would look,* they can say, *black people can't manage their own affairs.* Can't manage their own neighborhoods. So we good, God-fearing, kind, and merciful white folks *want to* help. Well, WE DON'T WANT ANY HELP. We'll do it ourselves. My house—and my blood—are not for sale."

Nedra was fierce. She talked about schools, talked about after-school programs, talked about nonexistent supermarkets, talked about medical clinics, brutally disparaged the many marijuana dispensaries. Like Du Bois on the export of gin to Africa. Keep the darkies stoned. Pliable. Complacent.

Nedra had made me read Du Bois. Made me read Frederick Douglass.

Then her segment was concluded. I snapped the TV off. *Whew.* Undoubtedly, Nedra and her interview had frightened the whole of L.A.'s Westside. Had raised the battered prices of all Los Angeles real estate north of Pico Boulevard. Things went dark below Pico.

Managers of gated communities everywhere leapt to their computers, rubbed their palms, conjured up raises in association fees.

From Pearly's commentary on gated communities, "Seven Keys":

> *She showed me the seven keys*
> *she needed to get in*
> *in the middle of the night*
> *she had no doubt*
> *high security is fine I said*
> *it must ease your mind in bed*
> *does it take those seven keys*
> *to get back out?*

Nedra Scott had been the most extraordinary woman I'd ever known. Physically she was gorgeous. To me. But that almost didn't matter. Her mind was infinitely agile, her choice of words exquisite, her deadpan delivery timeless, her scathing eye a source of delight. And she liked me! Genuinely liked me. We were on the same team. I was flattered, I was proud. For a time, my time with her, I was a larger human being than I'd ever been, before or since.

And she'd been mine. Had lain in my arms. Breathed with me the rarefied air of heaven itself. But, long ago, goodbye to all that.

Goodbye to all that.

CHAPTER FIFTEEN

Nothing Wrong with Him

But you couldn't keep even a Nedra in mind with a Puss by your side. Two nights later, Kiyoko maintaining her distance, Puss and I were in the dispatch office of the Gas Company. In the lot behind us were 250 Gas Company vans. Tom Thomason, who owed me one, dangled a set of keys in front of my face.

"This makes us even, Dick," said Tom.

"Even Steven." I had settled a small matter for Tom. I reached for the keys but he pulled them back.

"Don't kill anybody, dude," he admonished, "I'll get demerits on my employee review card."

We all laughed.

In the van, we changed into Gas Company uniforms and set out for Temescal Canyon. Puss lit up a cigarette and put her feet up on the dash.

"Thank you, Dick. This means a lot to me. I'll be good, I promise."

She'd said that every time. She didn't mean it to be bullshit.

But this time it would be pretty straightforward. Lewis would be there or not there. He'd either just tell her it was over, or he'd have left a nice little gift for her and she'd know it was over. Then she'd get drunk, but that wouldn't be my problem.

Suddenly my mind was on Georgette and all that I'd blown. In hindsight, for the most trivial of reasons. Because I'd desired two incompatible states. I'd wanted a wife and my fun, too. I hadn't been careful enough and now I was a satellite to a distant sun. But my children still loved me.

Children. In whose eyes you could still imagine an earthly paradise. But then they grew up. Ten years of age was the last time your children would think you were a better man than you were. So, in order to cushion their inevitable disappointment, you tried to be better. For as long as you could.

What would my descendants be doing as I set off on this profitless mission? Randy would be playing video games or watching *The Fifth Element* for the fiftieth time, or maybe, though I doubted it, he'd be reading those Edgar Rice Burroughs books I'd gotten for him. The Mars series. I loved Ghek, the hideous Kaldane.

Georgette would be reading Martine a Beatrix Potter story. *The Tale of Two Bad Mice.* Hunca Munca and Tom Thumb. My personal favorite among Miss Potter's excellent works. I'd read it twenty times to Randy. When the enraged mice destroyed the plaster food—I'd've done the same thing. Shortcut Mice.

I looked over at Puss. "Puss, did I leave my lighter at your house the other night?"

"What night?"

"That night. Two nights ago."

"The Zippo from Georgette?"

"I guess I did."

"You did."

The moon was fractured on the ocean and I was starting to feel sorry for myself when Puss started giving directions. I made a right at Temescal Canyon, then a turn this way and a turn that way and there we were.

A ten-foot masonry wall overflowing with bougainvillea surrounded the enclave. Some people had houses, some had apartments, some lived in their vehicles—this place was an enclave.

"What's the plan, Dick?"

Plan? Other than your disillusionment? "Look, either Art will be here or he won't. If something feels funny we'll take a quick look around if we can. But don't expect a lot."

"What does that mean?"

"It means we'll listen to what people say and evaluate it." Suddenly I found myself hoping this wouldn't be a disaster. I wouldn't let it. I turned to Puss. "We're *listening*. Nothing more."

"Listening for clues."

"That's right." Clues. Like the Hardy Boys. "And that's all." Like Nancy Drew.

I rolled the van up to the gate, pushed the button. After a bit, I heard a click and then a voice.

"Yes?" It was female.

"Gas Company for Mr. Lewis."

"Gas Company?"

"As scheduled. Open the gate, please."

"Uhhh . . ."

Pussy whispered at me. "That's the lady who answers at night. Who won't put me through."

"Mr. Lewis isn't available right now," said the voice. The voice had a spinsterish quality. I imagined a bitter, fiftyish woman, chain-smoking behind leaferous, ovate spectacles.

"Fine," I said. "But we need a signature. Can you come to the gate?"

"Why do you need a signature?"

"For the waiver."

"Waiver?"

"Stating we were here at such-and-such a time." I paused for emphasis. "And made warning."

There was a pause.

"Warning? What warning?"

"The paperwork says your water heaters are gas-operated. Anyway, some of those models, uh, like yours, uh, they, uh, have safety concerns. If you know what I mean."

"What do you mean?"

"I guess what I mean is that I hope you have plenty of fire insurance."

"Fire?"

"Well, uh, not in all cases."

The gate swung open, Puss gave me the thumbs-up.

We drove up the circular driveway to the front of the house. A woman in a nurse's hat with a green stripe was waiting at the front door.

"I'm Eileen Klasky, RN." She was mid-thirties, pretty in a hard-looking way, dark-headed. She looked at us suspiciously.

"Hi," I said. "I'm Dave Hunter. And this"—I indicated Pussy, who had her hair tied back and carried a clipboard—"is Gas Technician Williams."

"I guess you want to see the water heaters."

"Yes, ma'am. There're more than one?"

Nurse Klasky was brusque. "This house has seven bathrooms."

"Probably two or three heaters, then. Maybe an auxiliary upstairs." I ran my fingers through my hair. "We gonna scare anybody pokin' around?"

"Just the sick man upstairs."

Pussy immediately screwed up. "What's wrong with him?"

Klasky drew back. "Why would that be any of your business?"

"Sorry," said Puss.

"Fine." She looked at Puss astringently. "Can I show you to the basement, where the heaters are, or do you want to give the man upstairs a prostate massage?"

74

"Sorry," said Puss, again.

"We're just interested in the heaters, ma'am." I looked sternly at Puss.

"Then follow me."

The sick man upstairs. Lewis was sick and that was all there was to it. But the charade had to conclude in character.

A staircase at the rear of the entryway led down. The basement was extensive and well finished. Finally we reached the utility room.

Four huge water heaters were bolted to the wall. They shared space with a set of dining room chairs, some random pieces of furniture, a couple of birdcages, some floor lamps, and some saggy cardboard boxes.

I examined the heaters, checked my clipboard, nodded. "Yup. These are the ones." I looked at Puss. "You ready to take some numbers?"

"Yes, I am." She readied her clipboard. She was seldom as compliant in real life.

I got down on one knee, started reading some numbers, whatever they meant. "G-c-3-4-654-PRL-18. Got that?"

"Wait a second."

Wait a second? That meant she was thinking. I looked at her and she was looking at me. Something was up.

She came over. "That number doesn't sound right." She pointed to some writing on her clipboard.

I have to go upstairs and see.

"That's impossible." I looked into her eyes. She pleaded silently. What to do?

I punted. "Let me check the number one more time." Again I bent down and read. "G-c-3-4-654-PRL-18. No, that's PRL-*19*."

"That makes it right."

I decided to let her go up. Maria and Victor, the usual staff, who Puss had told me about, would take no surprise in her presence. "Go out to the truck," I instructed. "See if you can find the replacement parts. We may have the whole subassembly on board."

That would get her a minute or two if I could distract the nurse.

I have to go upstairs and see. I thoroughly crossed out Puss's note.

I turned to the nurse, proffered the clipboard. "Could you take a few numbers down, ma'am? We'll be out of your hair that much quicker."

With a sigh of irritation she took the clipboard. "For Christ's sake."

Pussy signaled that she was leaving. "I'm going to go upstairs to the truck, Dick."

"Fine. And you may as well check online. And hurry. We're making the lady wait."

Pussy was gone in a flash.

Klasky tipped her head to one side. "I thought you said your name was Dave."

It was until Pussy forgot her lines.

"Dick, Dave, what's the difference?" I shrugged, got down and looked for another number. I'd bluff my way through.

"Your name is Dick-Dave?"

Sweet Christ. Now I was a hayseed.

"That's my name, Dick-Dave. Call me whatever you want. Or either one."

Penelope Grafton, a.k.a. Pussy Grace, reached the entryway, listened. The house was quiet. Her heart was beating at hyperspeed. It was now or never. She turned and raced upstairs.

The door of the master suite was open. She slowed and entered on tiptoe. The room, usually exceptionally neat, was helter-skelter.

On the bed, under a haphazard mass of covers, a large form breathed heavily.

She approached, pulled the covers back.

Art. But, Jesus Christ. He was many days unshaven, and very pale. His breath came irregularly, there were dried liquids at the corners of his mouth. He was wearing filthy, wrinkled pajamas and smelled of urine. His breath was foul, medicinal.

On his bedside table were a multitude of prescription bottles and random tablets of different sizes and colors. Art had *never* been sick.

Art groaned, scaring her, and his eyes opened. They were unfocused, looked past her. He finally saw her, tried to sit up, talk.

"Uhhgg. Prushy . . ."

"Art! Are you alright?"

He fell back into his pillow.

"Art, what's happened? Are you okay?"

Art, with great effort, sat up. He saw his table of medicines, knocked them explosively to the floor. "All shfucked up, Prushy. Shelp me."

When would stupid Pussy Grace come back down here and rescue me from the bad theater I was stuck in? She'd done it again. And I'd let her do it. *Shit.* Meanwhile I lay on my back, neck twisted like a giraffe, with a flashlight, reading meaningless numbers to Nursie. "T-15-fg-431-plu-23-a. Got it?"

"Got it, Dick-Dave."

Fucking Dick-Dave. I would kill Puss.

"Wait a second," said Nursie.

"What?"

"*B*-l-u or *p*-l-u?"

"Uhhhh . . . *p*-l-u." The flashlight was getting yellow and dim. I shook it.

"I thought so. Thanks, Dick-Dave."

She *thought* so. Was she fucking with me?

"It could have been *c*-l-u," enunciated Nursie, carefully.

"I see. But, as luck would have it, it's *p*-l-u."

"What's i-c?"

"What are you talking about?"

"You said 'i-c,' Dick-Dave."

"No, I didn't."

"You said, 'i-c, it's p-l-u.'"

"Then it's p-l-u." Goddamnit.

"I know that, Dick-Dave."

"Then what's the problem?"

"Let's start over."

Fuck me with a spoon I hated Puss and Nursie and their whole accursed sex. I moved my head to reread the placard and something metal and sharpish jabbed into my head behind my ear. God-*damnit*.

"Can you still see?"

"Yes." Of course I could see. If my flashlight hadn't, that second, cut out. I banged it again and it came back. I started reading numbers, eyes bulging with rage, in the yellowish dark. I read slowly. Like you'd read to a moron. If a moron insisted on being read to.

"T—15—fg—431—plu—23—a. Got it?"

"Of course I got it, Dick-Dave."

"You sure?"

"Sure I'm sure. It's what I had last time."

Pussy had never really appreciated how big Art was. He was huge and he was heavy. She felt like a bird leading a hippopotamus by a string. Who was walking whom was the question.

"I'm prishoner, Prushy. In a den of theiveths. They want my money."

He had one arm over her shoulder and she had an arm around his waist. He was unsteady on his feet. She wondered if she could keep him up.

"Are you through screwing around with those heaters?"

"Screwing around?"

"Screwing around."

I nodded. "I guess. For the most part."

"Then let's get a move on." She handed me the clipboard filled with nonsense. "Where's your brainless assistant?"

I shrugged. That's what I wanted to know: Where *was* my brainless assistant? "Still in the truck, I guess." I'd have to screw around a little longer. "It's time to purge the heaters," I said.

He was walking a little stronger. He was coming back. Her hand pushed into the small of his back. She encouraged him. "That's it, hon. That's it. All we gotta do is find a way to get you out of here."

But suddenly Art had stopped dead in his tracks. With his huge fists clenched, he stared upward, trembling violently. From his throat came a terrible shout of pure agony. She pushed against his back but there was no way she could keep him up. Slowly, like a massive tree, he toppled backward and smashed to the floor.

I heard the scream and the thud and I knew things were severely fucked up in a brand-new way. Nursie ran for the stairs and I followed her up.

The master suite was full of refuse and there in the middle of the floor lay a huge man on his back.

"Goddamnit." Nursie threw herself down, pushed an eye open, checked for a pulse at the neck.

I looked down. Lewis looked very dead to me.

Nursie started in on CPR. A breath. Five chest compressions. A breath. She looked up at me. "Call . . ." Then stopped.

What else but 911? "I'll call 911," I said, pulling out my phone.

But then Pussy stepped out of the shadows, a cane in her hands. "Don't bother. He's dead."

Nursie spun to Pussy's voice. Pussy swung the cane like a bat, whacked Nursie across the side of the head. Nursie fell across Lewis, unconscious.

I didn't know whether to shit or wind my watch. I wanted to kill Puss. "What the FUCK? You *idiot*."

I dragged Nursie off Lewis. "Help her. She'd better be fucking alive."

I took Nursie's place with Art. One breath. Five compressions.

Puss examined Nursie. "This bitch is alright."

Panting, I raised myself from Lewis. "Maybe that bitch is his nurse, you moron."

I did another two minutes on Lewis. Nothing. The man was cashed out.

Puss looked over. "He was dead when he hit the ground."

"Fuck you, doctor."

"He was dead, Dick, I could tell."

Nursie moaned. Which meant she was about to be a problem.

"What are we going to do with her?" I asked. It was a rhetorical question.

Before I could stop her, Puss whacked her with the cane again. Right across the forehead. Nursie went limp again.

"God DAMN it." I pointed to the corner of the room. "Go over there and sit. Don't do anything more. Don't move. Just sit."

I checked Nursie out. Still alive. Thank God. I dragged her over to Lewis's bed, laid her there.

"She'll be alright," said Puss.

"*Fuck. You.* Just sit there."

I tried to think. What was I in the middle of, so far? Trespassing, home invasion, assault, manslaughter. And conspiracy.

"I had him up and then he fell," volunteered Puss.

"But *why* did you have him up, doctor? If you don't mind me asking."

"There was nothing wrong with him."

I pointed to the corpse.

"Obviously. Nothing wrong with him."

"They were drugging him. He was a prisoner."

"You don't know that."

"Yes, I *do*. He told me. And I *was* a nurse."

"You? A nurse?"

"Yes, butthead." Then, an amendment. "Almost."

"A wet nurse."

"El Camino Community College."

I looked around the disaster site. Nursie stirred again. "We gotta get out of here. What did you touch?"

"Everything," said Puss.

Gauging my luck, I half-expected the gate not to work. But it opened right up. I rolled down the hill, made a left at PCH. I heard no sirens, saw no flashing lights. I zapped the window down, breathed the ocean air.

"I'm sorry, Dick. I'm really sorry."

There were no words in the English language that could adequately express my disappointment in myself. And all I knew was English.

Puss persisted. "Dick, I'm sorry."

"Shut up."

As we approached Entrada Drive and Patrick's Roadhouse, of

Schwarzenegger fame, a yellow Mercedes took the corner, coming toward us on two wheels.

"I've always hated those things," editorialized Puss. "And the bitches who drive them."

I was still beyond words.

"Don't you hate them, too?"

"Shut up, Puss. Just. Shut. Up."

CHAPTER SIXTEEN

Sisters

Ellen Glidden was at Art Lewis's house fourteen minutes later. "It's me, idiot," she snarled into the security box, "open up." The gate rolled back.

Upstairs, in the master suite, she looked down on dead Art Lewis. She turned to her sister. "You stupid goat. Ask you to do *anything*. All you had to do was fucking watch him. It was that simple. But no."

Ellen poked the toe of her pointed leather shoe into the corpse's side. "Wake up, asshole." She knelt down and pushed back an eyelid. No response. Shit. Disaster. Fucking Art Lewis. Beyond earthly concerns.

She looked around the room. "Who else was here?"

Eileen despised herself at that moment. Even more than she hated and feared her elder sister. When Ellen had called a week ago with a surefire way for her to make twenty-five thousand dollars, in cash, she should have hung up the phone. Instead she listened. And earlier this evening, watching *Law & Order,* she realized that keeping Mr. Lewis drugged up in his own home was a special kind of kidnapping.

"I asked who else was here."

Eileen flared. "Goddamnit, Ellen. Who died and made you king? No one was here."

"I saw a ball cap in the entryway, Eileen. Art Lewis didn't wear ball caps and it wasn't there this morning."

Eileen folded. "The Gas Company came. They were making a safety check."

"So you just let them in."

"It was the Gas Company, Ellen."

"What did I tell you? No more calls, no entries."

"It was the Gas Company, Ellen. It would have raised suspicion not letting them in."

"You looked at their identification?"

"Yes."

"*Liar.*"

"They were here to check the water heaters. It was let them inspect"—she spread her hands suggesting the reasonableness of her actions—"or sign a waiver saying I refused the check. I didn't think you'd want me signing anything."

Ellen stared at her sister. Supposedly from the same parents. An imbecile of the first water. "You didn't give me *thought one.* Because you have no thoughts. You read the waiver?"

"Uh, no."

"Of course not. Where did they go?"

"To the water heaters in the basement. They took numbers down."

"Both of them?"

"One of them did go back to the truck."

"And you followed that person?"

"No."

"So you don't know *where* they went."

"The guy stayed in the basement. I watched him like a hawk. The girl went back to the truck to—"

"The girl?"

"A woman. Mid-thirties, I'd say."

Eileen could never tolerate Ellen's rage. Her earliest memories were of Ellen mad. Those burning eyes making her brain smoke. She could feel it in the center of her head as she sucked lies and falsehoods from the ether to placate the evil witch. "After the guy took down the numbers I took him back to the entryway. Then I heard a thud and I ran up here."

Eileen pointed to the corpse. "And he was right where he is now." She swallowed. "And then the girl came out of nowhere and hit me in the head."

"*What?*"

"She hit me with a cane."

"That's why there's that lump on your forehead."

"Yes."

"So *everyone* was up here and saw the dead man?"

"I guess so."

Ellen blew up. "You are too stupid to live. The next thing you'll say is everyone was gone and then you called me."

"That's what happened."

Ellen looked around the room, thought. She put another toe into Art's side. Nothing. The big asshole was dead. "They couldn't have been Gas Company employees."

"I don't know."

"Of course they weren't, you goat. Gas Company employees don't assault their customers with canes." She looked at the egg over her sister's left eye. "Put some ice on that thing."

The sisters straightened up the bedroom as best they could, cleaned all surfaces with 409. The drugs were put into a plastic bag to be disposed of. But Art was just too heavy to move. He must have weighed four hundred pounds. Asshole.

"What do we do now?" whined Eileen.

"I don't know." It depended on who Eileen's visitors were. Then Ellen remembered the security shack. It wasn't locked. She fiddled, could only find the front-door footage.

"Are there cameras all over the house?"

"Sixty of them. They're everywhere. Catching everything. You blow the gas man or something?"

"Don't be disgusting," said Eileen.

Ellen got the front-door footage up on the monitor. The video looked over Eileen's shoulder down on two figures, a man and a woman. Good sweet Christ. Relief filled her like cool water.

"These are the two?"

"Yes."

Ellen lit up a cigarette. "Well, luckily for you, I know that woman. That's Art's girlfriend. Her name is Pussy Grace." A no-account pole dancer. She wouldn't want to get involved. Wouldn't call the police.

"And who's he?"

"Don't know him." Yes, Pussy Grace meant amateur hour and that meant everything wasn't ruined. Pussy was suspicious, that's why she came snooping, but she didn't have enough brain wattage to light a match. Ellen sucked in another draft of nicotine. Everything could still work out.

CHAPTER SEVENTEEN

Opportunity Rings

Bobby had just exhaled a fragrant cloud of purple smoke when the phone rang. Who the hell would be calling at this hour? No friend would be calling so late. He had no friends anyway. Didn't need any fucking friends. Because, in the drawer under the tabletop, he had everything a man might possibly need, more than a friend might provide. A full ounce of cocaine.

On the second set of rings he looked at the phone to see who it might be. E. Glidden. That bitch.

"This better be good," he answered.

"How'd you like to make fifty grand?"

"Who do I gotta kill?"

"He's already dead."

Hmmm. Interesting.

Very interesting. Now he was driving to Temescal Canyon in his green Infiniti 335, the only remnant of his old life. Fifty for a night's work. That was his style. Mr. Bobby Lebow style. He reached over, into the leather valise on the passenger seat, felt for the bag of small rocks. There it was. He relaxed.

CHAPTER EIGHTEEN

Spontaneous Combustion

I woke up the next morning with a low, shitty feeling in every cell of my body, the sword of what's-his-name right over my head. I heard sirens in the canyon but they weren't for me. Yet.

I had one more Nedra Scott detail to accomplish before the authorities descended. For a honeybee in the right hand, information I had requested yesterday had been procured. I now had the personal cell phone number of Robert Patrick, the heavy cheese behind Azure Gardens, LLC.

He picked up on the second ring. "This is Bob."

"Hi, Bob. This is Dick Henry."

A hesitation.

"Do I know you, Mr. Henry?"

"Now you do."

"You got twenty seconds."

"That's all I need. I represent Nedra Scott. From Bledsoe. This is a warning. If your goons mess with her again, or even look at her funny, I'll be holding you personally responsible. You got that?"

"I don't know who you are and I resent the implication that I have—"

I realized I had a blinding headache. "Cut the shit, Bob. I'm only going to tell you this one time. Lay off Nedra Scott or *you pay.* Personally. You got me?"

"Listen, here. I'm calling the authorities—"

"The authorities can't help you, Bob. I got your personal phone number, I know your address, I could walk into your bedroom tonight. I know what's on your bedside table. This is between you and me. Now, you can offer Ms. Scott any price you like, who knows what she might accept, but the threats from you and your goons are over. You understand me?"

"Listen—"

"You listen. And understand me, Bob the Knob, of 271 Charing Cross Road." I could hear him breathe. "Don't fuck up now. My name's Dick Henry. They call me the Shortcut Man. Ask your friends about me."

I hung up, found some ibuprofen in the medicine cabinet. Swallowed two blue capsules. The phone rang. Good. That would be my new friend, Bob the Knob.

It was Puss.

"Dick?"

"I'm sorry, but *fuck you,* Puss. Don't call me ever again. *Ever.*"

"Turn on Channel Nine."

"No."

"Turn on Channel Nine right now. It has to do with you-know-what. Turn it on. I'll call you back."

I had to turn it on. It was a low-rent local duo, Bill Devers and Barbara Barnes.

"Welcome back," said Devers. "And now for a little happy news. Let's turn to Barbara Barnes."

Let's.

Barbara had a pretty face, a nice rack, all her teeth, and could read English in a loud, clear voice. The only qualifications a female newsreader need possess. "Thank you, Bill. Well, clear the decks, everybody. Yesterday one of L.A.'s most eligible bachelors went down in a blaze of matrimony."

Art Lewis came up on the screen.

"Art Lewis, famed developer and philanthropist, married Eileen Klasky, sister of TV star Ellen Havertine."

I stopped breathing.

"Havertine is currently married to the Honorable Harold J. Glidden, who sits on the Los Angeles Superior Court. The superprivate nuptial ceremonies were held at the Temescal Canyon home of Lewis. The honeymoon is under way but the location has not been revealed to this reporter."

I met Puss in the old section of the Farmers Market. We shared a pot of coffee as a Laotian immigrant mangled order numbers for French pancakes. Again, I was reminded the English language is not owned by the eggheads who create expensive textbooks. It's owned by its speakers around the world.

"Maybe he's really alive," said Puss.

"No, he isn't. He's dead."

"It's called spontaneous combustion, Dick."

"No, it's not called spontaneous combustion." *Jesus.*

"Yes, it is. I learned it at El Camino."

"No, you didn't. And it didn't happen. Art is dead."

"So he's not married."

"He may be married but he doesn't know it. It was a posthumous ceremony."

"Maybe, but he was probably dead."

"Yeah, Puss." I wasn't going to be able to put this one completely across.

Then I saw tears rolling down her cheeks. I put my hand over hers. "I'm sorry, Puss. I'm sorry."

"I loved him, Dick. And he loved me. In his way. I know he did. Don't you think so?"

"I'm sure of it, dear."

Puss sobbed and I let her roll. I was so shell-shocked I hadn't even thought of the way Puss must have felt. I was too busy imagining the Graybar Hotel.

Poor Puss. How many souls do we allow into our lives in our lifetime anyway? Not only does the process become harder and harder as time goes by, there are precious few to begin with. We overcome the flinch response, we suspend disbelief, and every once in a while we taste glory.

Goodbye to all that. And then you die. But fuck this, or I'll need a double Stoli and a shot of heroin.

Puss had recovered her composure somewhat. She wiped her eyes, tried to smile.

"Did you recognize the woman he married?" I asked her.

"Ellen Havertine's sister."

"You know her."

"I do?"

"Yeah. You whacked her in the head with a cane."

"That bitch?"

Yeah, Puss. That bitch.

The news of Lewis's marriage told me one good thing. I wouldn't have to wait for the authorities to roust me. The authorities hadn't a whiff. Because a conspiracy was afoot.

Of the three people mentioned in the media, I put the Havertine lady at the center of things. Her sister, Dick-Dave Eileen, couldn't have been the brains of the operation. She didn't *have* the brains. Or the drive. The *L.A. Times* had reported that Judge Glidden performed the ceremony. That wasn't happenstance. He would be part of the conspiracy, too.

I thought about our lunch at the Pantry. Glidden was vain. Vanity would make him susceptible to the pressure to maintain appearances. Grand appearances. Especially to look good for a younger wife. And what would make a judge cross the line so egregiously? Opportunity. Clear opportunity and the pressure from a young, indignant wife in the face of expensive tastes, diminished income. I bet the Gliddens were broke. I would send a honeybee downtown and have it checked out.

What did the Kostabi have to do with anything?

Nothing that I could see. It stood on its own. Maybe. I don't trust coincidence.

Where did Puss and I fit in? The fact that we had not called the police told the Havertine clique that our presence at the house was not aboveboard either, certainly not the Gas Company. We were mystery people on the other side of the same plot. They'd be waiting for us to claim a share. More than waiting. They'd be looking for us.

PART TWO

Bambi Service

CHAPTER NINETEEN

The Tale of Hi-Beam

Blue Monday rolled around, so it was time for me to drop off some checks. I parked in front of the little house on South Arden Boulevard I used to call home, rang the bell, and waited.

If all marriages started with divorce they might last a little longer. Because you'd know the adversary up front. For good or for evil.

Georgette opened the door. She cleverly restrained her good nature. "You."

"The one and only."

"Did you bring money?"

I pulled two checks out of my pocket, she plucked them from my fingers.

"How are my little people?"

"They're asleep."

No sooner had these pearls dropped from her lips than my daughter, Martine, appeared. Skipping. I loved her five thousand different ways and my heart leapt.

"Hello, little love," I said, and she rushed into my arms. One of her hugs went a long way. Had to go a long way.

Georgette looked down. "What are you doing up?"

"I heard Daddy's voice."

Yes. *Daddy's* voice. And only I, Dick Henry, possessed it.

Georgette shrugged. "I guess it's not too late."

I set Martine down. "It's never too late, is it, darling?"

"Sometimes it is," said Martine, seriously.

"Really. When?"

"When it's already too late."

Wow. Led into philosophical thickets by a seven-year-old.

She moved on to code. "X-Y-Z, Daddy."

I certainly didn't know what that meant. I looked to Georgette. She knew as much as I did. "What's X-Y-Z, dear?"

Martine shook her head in a world-weary manner. Directly inherited from her mother. Her hands went to her hips. "Examine Your Zipper, Dad."

I looked down, zipped up. "Sorry."

"Someone should have told you."

"Someone should've." I apologized with a spread of hands.

Martine's eyes glinted with mischief. "Tell me the dead cat story again, Daddy."

Both of the kids loved the dead cat story. I looked at Georgette. *If you must,* she expressed without words.

Actually, I knew three dead cat stories. And one Texas-small-town tale I'd heard in the Navy about how to make a cat into a bagpipe.

How to make a cat into a bagpipe:

1) Catch stray cat.

2) Put cat into paper bag.

3) Orient bag so cat's head is clamped in armpit, legs pointing down.

4) Place cat's tail between your teeth (molars).

5) "Tune" cat by manipulating hind leg (avoid claws).

6) Bite down on tail, rhythmically.

7) Enjoy the tuneful yowling.

*   *   *

One cat may be cruelty. Two, a novelty. Three, a statistic. Five, a parade.

So, the dead cat story. "Once upon a time there was a cat."

"A cat with one eye," interjected Martine, obsessive with detail. "Just a kitten."

"Yes. A cat with one eye. Just a kitten. Now *what* was his name?"

"His name was Hi-Beam."

"That's right. Hi-Beam."

Hi-Beam's tale was this. After Georgette and I were married, our first home had been a small attachment to a larger house. We had no yard. But, by informal agreement with our neighbor, our landlord had secured us, across a low wall, use of a tiny back corner of the neighbor's property. The neighbor's house and seemingly all her personal items were purple. Purple doormat. Purple wheelbarrow with purple flowers.

Our fiefdom consisted of a few square feet of mossy ground, three scraggly rose bushes, a failing jacaranda, some stepping-stones, and a small, gasping fountain. But it was enough for Georgette and me in our happy first days. And it was enough for Hi-Beam.

On Thanksgiving Day, Hi-Beam walked into Alma Avenue and got squashed. Maybe it was the one-eye thing. But his pouncing days were over. Georgette and I were brokenhearted. Now what to do with his remains? The trash barrel seemed heartless. Our landlord's property was essentially concrete. So it looked like the garden.

I knocked on the door of the purple house but the purple lady was not home. I would talk to her later. We went ahead with our little ceremony in the garden. *May noble Hi-Beam be rejoined to the Great Spirit. From whom he parted such a short time ago. Amen.* A shoebox-size grave was shallowly excavated and refilled.

That should have been the end of the story. I never did get around to informing the purple lady what I had done on her property, getting her belated permission. Though I had fully intended to do so. Admittedly, it might have been awkward. After the interment and all. I should have called Ravenich.

Four months later, to joyously accommodate her daughter's baby shower, purple lady had the grounds of her property redone. The scraggly rosebushes had to go. New purple roses would be planted. By wretched luck, a shallow depression in the backyard was chosen for a planting site.

When the Mexican garden team penetrated Hi-Beam's grave all hell broke loose. I was not on scene.

Georgette called me to explain that a posse of gardeners had electrified the neighborhood with their shrieks and supplications for the mercy of God. Purple lady started shrieking, too. Soon police arrived. And more police. And more police. Maybe a child had been buried in the garden. Aspects of Monte Cristo. On a dark and stormy night. A premature child. A freak. Smothered. A premature freak child with a tail.

Reason was restored with the arrival of the second fire unit, the hook and ladder. "Looks like a fuckin' cat," commented unamused Firefighter Garcia, wheelman, ejecting a stream of tobacco juice into the fresh-turned earth. Unless the little bastard had fur. And whiskers.

Georgette had been questioned by the constabulary. What do you know about this?

You mean about the burial in the backyard?

How did you know it was a burial?

I didn't know. And I still don't.

Georgette was a terrible liar. But she stuck to her story. Finally, Earl, who lived across the street, settled the matter, walking away with a small plastic bag, ending the controversy.

It was the procedural monkeyfuck that delighted the children. "How many police cars?" asked Martine, ready to explode with mirth.

"Seven." The number had grown in the retelling.

"And how many fire trucks?"

"Twelve."

Martine rolled on the floor and kicked her feet. "And how many gardeners?" she quavered.

"Twenty-three." A cast of thousands.

Georgette looked at me, tapped her watch.

I looked into the eyes of my beloved daughter. Next time I told the tale it would be longer. Maybe Animal Control would get involved. But now it was time to go.

Martine regained her feet, out of breath. She came and hugged me. Her dear little hands. "I love you, Daddy."

"And Daddy loves you, too, little girl. Next time maybe he'll stay a little longer and ask you what you've been up to."

"Oh, I've been playing Barbie."

Barbie. If only I'd been smart enough to invent her. "Barbie's cool."

"Barbie has impossible figures. Her legs are too long."

"Actually, darling, long legs are never a problem." Part of the Shortcut Man's worldview.

"And her casabas are too big."

A shadow crossed my good mood. Indoctrination. I smelled indoctrination. Like cat urine. I eyed Georgette. "Casabas? Isn't it a little early to be filled with . . . with this kind of stuff?"

"The truth is never too early," said Georgette. Coldly.

"We saw you today, Daddy."

"*You did?* Where? You didn't say hello?"

"At Farmers Market. You were with your new girlfriend. The one with big casabas."

I looked sternly at my ex. "I think you're talking about one of Daddy's clients."

"You were holding hands across the table, Dad."

Puss in extremis. "Well, dear, she was—"

"I know what she is," stated my daughter, an infant once removed.

"You do? What is she?"

"She's a pole dancer."

"A *what?*"

"Why don't you run along to bed, sweetheart?" said Georgette, a fixed smile on her face.

Martine gave me another kiss and scampered off.

I turned to Georgette. "What the *hell* is happening around here? You get religion or something? Casabas? *Pole dancer?* Aren't we laying things on a little thick?"

"That woman was built like a pole dancer, Dick."

"Well, you're wrong. Way wrong."

"What is she?"

Let's see. "She's a scientist."

"A *scientist?*"

We hung there, precariously, for a moment.

Then conversation resumed. Georgette folded her arms. "Speaking for the more modestly endowed, Dick, I don't know that Barbie worship is a good thing."

"Can't she just grow up? Like you did? For Christ's sake."

"To make choices like I did?"

"You made some good ones."

"And you weren't one of them, Dick."

I felt that cold adversarial anger rising within me. "My children are my testimonial, dear."

"Possibly."

"Possibly?"

"Maybe they're the milkman's testimonial."

I took a deep breath, smiled with all the dignity I could summon. "On those fragrant words, *you mammal,* I'll be pushing on."

*　　*　　*

I reran the conversation all the way to Pacific Palisades. Only in the narrowest technical terms could I declare victory. *Mammal*. Fuck it. It was Kiyoko I really wanted to see.

Lovely Kiyoko. There was a little flower shop out there. Maybe I'd surprise her with a big fistful of carnations, her favorite.

Or maybe they weren't her favorite. Kiyoko would know carnations are budget flowers, a friend of mine, Anna, had told me. Maybe she's going easy on your wallet.

In other words, Kiyoko thought I was some poor, penny-ante waste of skin. Okay. Maybe I'd spring for an orchid.

I went Sunset all the way but the flower place was out of business. But, having gone that far, I decided fate had determined I knock on her door anyway.

Empty-handed, I smiled winningly. Illuminated by the porch light, she had two words for me.

Get out.

Actually, three words.

Get out. Barbarian.

CHAPTER TWENTY

Honeymoon on Ice

Ellen knocked and heard Bobby get up. The door opened and she went in. After a point, a place got no messier. There was no way to tell.

Bobby went back to his seat behind the coffee table. He grinned. "They'll let anyone get married these days."

Ellen shrugged, sat down. "It was Eileen or nothing."

"Pretty smart. But nothing might have tempted *me*. You didn't mention the change to Erin Halle."

"Not yet."

"Who knew the old fuck would marry a goat."

"Thanks for your help last night."

"I love a honeymoon on ice."

Bobby poured a gram of coke into the vial and added a thumbnail of baking soda. "How about a hit, Mrs. Glidden?"

"Sure."

Bobby swirled the tube, cooking it with the Bic. Crystals formed, sank to the bottom.

Bobby grinned. "Does the judge know his wife likes to smoke a little crack now and then?"

"Of course. He loves the idea."

"Where's the bride?"

"Stashed. In the desert. With the Indians."

"She belongs in the desert." Bobby poured off the water, rolled out the crack sludge onto a CD. Fuck the tomahawk. The Indians had triumphed over the white man with bingo and blackjack. Who could have guessed? While Black Elk had returned to the Great Spirit grieving.

Bobby troweled two pipes, slid one over to Ellen. "Bon appetit."

Ellen's gong was rung. "Ohhh, that's good."

"You bet it is. I know how to cook, baby."

Ellen slid Bobby her pipe for a refill. "There's something I've got to tell you about last night."

Bobby put down the pipes. "Goddamnit. The tell-Bobby-later syndrome. As *always*. What is it this time?"

"Nothing vital."

"How not vital?"

"There were some phony Gas Company employees at Art's house last night. Before you came over last night."

"What?"

"Eileen let them in."

"While he was dead?"

"Yes."

Bobby picked up a can of beer, threw it across the room. It hit the wall, splashed. "God *damn* it. That's fuckin' beautiful. And you don't think to tell me that before I come over there? That's fuckin' huge. I wouldn't've come over."

"It's not as bad as all that, Bobby."

"But they saw him . . . dead?"

"Yes."

"Christ *Jesus*. We're fucked, in other words."

"I don't think so. They weren't real Gas Company people. And I've ID'd one of them."

"Out of how many?"

"There were two of them. One of them was Art's girlfriend. Her name's Pussy Grace. She's a stripper. I had dinner with her and Art a couple of weeks ago."

"Pussy Grace. Phony name. And the other? A guy?"

Ellen nodded. "I don't know him. But he's on the surveillance tape."

"Who's the boss?"

"The stripper."

"Why do you think so?"

"Because she's the one who hit Eileen with the cane. She must be in charge."

"He's a lump, in other words. Transportation."

"That's what I think. He's a lump, Eileen *has* a lump."

Laughter.

"Why didn't you show me the surveillance tape when I was over there?"

"I wanted to do one thing at a time."

"Lying bitch. You just didn't want to tell me."

Ellen dug in her purse, pulled out a piece of paper. "This is her address."

Bobby took it. "Where'd you get it?"

"I was going to send her some classical dance tapes."

He studied it. "What does Bobby have to do now?"

"Go have a talk with her. Scare the crap out of her. Make her think that Art's death could be blamed on her."

"I can do that." He packed his pipe. "For a price."

"You made fifty thousand last night."

He lit up. "Pay me."

"Bobby."

"Pay me." He exhaled.

"I can't pay you tonight. You know that."

"Oh well."

"Bobby. Help me."

"Okay. But now I'm a partner, not a handyman."

"Okay. You're a partner."

"I want a mil. When this is all through."

"Okay."

"A million dollars. Say it."

"A million dollars. When we're done. Now here's the address."

Bobby studied it. "Just over on Sierra Bonita."

"Right above Sunset."

"I'll roll over tomorrow afternoon." Bobby filled her pipe. "Have a hit before you split. Partner."

"Thank you, Mr. Lebow."

"You're welcome, Mrs. Glidden."

CHAPTER TWENTY-ONE

A Peach, a Plum, an Eggplant

My phone rang. Latrell. Things were going alright down there. Bosto Ket had shown up, waved a gun around, frightened off the thugs, tried out sweet words on Latrell's mother.

Sweet words. On Nedra. Bosto had failed?

Utterly and completely.

Latrell, feeling better overall, passed on greetings from barber Deakins. I returned Archie's salutations. How, inquired Latrell, had I met Archie?

Of course, it wasn't Latrell's business, so I told him about a large fish and the Santa Monica Pier and the finding of a gold watch.

Actually it had gone down like this. Archie, on my instruction, referred his blackmailer to his two silent partners, without whose blessing, he, Archie, claimed he could do nothing. The blackmailers, endorsing all stereotypes, met the silent partners after hours in the barbershop back room.

Stracewski and his torpedo were twenty minutes late. In light-colored garments, with visible chest hair and gold chains, they reeked of chutzpah and Miami Beach.

Gold Chain immediately fucked up. Taking in Rojas, the Mayan prince, Stracewski scratched his head, looked at me. "What's he here for, to mow the lawn?"

I didn't have to time to warn Gold Chain this was not the way to refer to a prince. Like a jaguar, Rojas was across the room in a single bound, delivering a vicious left hook to Stracewski's liver. Stracewski's liver signaled to the brain that the tongue had erred and the legs would no longer support the torso. Down went Stracewski with a ragged gasp of agony.

I met the torpedo coming to render aid. I was confident Torpedo was unaware he was about to meet the former light-heavyweight champion of the 13th Naval District. I feinted with a right and threw a left hook. It hit him in the exact same spot I'd hit Lance Corporal Charlton Parker years ago. With the same gratifying result. The body, deprived of management, waved its fists and fell down in the corner.

In a minute the two pliant gentlemen had been tied to chairs, hands behind them. Rojas held up a barber's mirror as I put a plastic fastener around Stracewski's neck and snugged it up.

Looking through his wallet, I removed all cash and cards. That's how I found out his name was Stracewski. "Do I have your attention, Mr. Stracewski?"

He motioned that I had his full attention. Meanwhile, the plastic tie started his slow suffocation. His face was taking on a reddish hue.

I smiled affably. "My friend, Mr. Deakins, stated that you had treated him with rudeness and disrespect. Is that true?"

Stracewski nodded that it was indeed the truth. That he was sorry for it.

I looked into Rojas's mirror, into Stracewski's eyes. "You're starting to look like a plum." The man was getting darker by the second. Purple. The color of contrition.

"Now, in order to facilitate your apology to Mr. Deakins, I'm going to confiscate your cash, which comes to a pitiful six hundred and twenty-three dollars. Is this alright with you?"

It was alright with him.

"And your credit cards and driver's license. I'm going to shred them. Does that meet with your approval?"

It did meet with his approval.

I indicated his somnolent assistant. "I'm also confiscating Torpedo's cash and shredding his documents. Does that meet with your approval?"

It did meet with his approval.

Now it was time for intimidating threats. Rojas read my mind. "Tell him about Johnny Santo, dude." Rojas grinned.

Like I've said, you couldn't be depressed in Rojas's company. "Mr. Stracewski, if you ever make an appearance on Hawthorne Boulevard again, in *Lennox,* it will be the last thing you do in this life. Is that clear?"

It was abundantly clear.

"In fact, if I hear your name again, you're dead. Have I made myself clear?"

Gold Chain nodded. Lack of oxygen had led directly to clarity.

Rojas grinned into the mirror at dark Stracewski. "You kinda look like a eggplant, dude."

He did look like an eggplant. A dark, rich purple. I snipped the tie with a pair of Archie's scissors and a wiser Stracewski sucked life back into his body.

Archie had come to me later, laughing. "I don't know what you done, but people be thinkin' I done it. Treatin' me like the Godfather and shit, know what I mean?"

Archie was sporting a new, white broadbrimmed hat. Fanuccistyle. He shook my hand. "Best five hundred dollars I ever spent." He nodded. "Shortcut Man. Gotta dig him."

Got to indeed.

Got to.

*   *   *

So you met Archie *fishing*? And you found a watch?

    Yes, Latrell. That's how I met him.

    In the fish. The watch was *in* the fish?

    That may have been going too far, but I was already committed.

Yes, Latrell. The watch was in the fish.

CHAPTER TWENTY-TWO

Anger Management

From the Cherokee to the guitar district was just a few minutes. Down Cherokee to Sunset, and right. Past a couple of heroin motels, Social Security, and Hollywood High.

Then the guitar district. Which meant something different to Mr. Bobby Lebow. He'd been through the crucible of fame. Though it didn't feel like a crucible when you were in it. It felt a like a well-deserved warm bath. With dozens of happy lackeys, eyes shyly on the floor, ready to hand you towels of infinite softness. Fame wasn't the arrival after an arduous journey, it was the recognition by the world of your remarkable inner spirit. And once recognized, you humbly took your place in the pantheon, where you would remain for eternity. Except that you didn't.

A long time ago he'd been a normal twelve-year-old in seventh grade at St. Ambrose School. Mary Tyler Moore had been a student there. So what. The school, as a school, conferred nothing extraordinary besides the fact that CBS Television City was right down the street. Which, in Bobby's case, was enough.

The class had been invited down to see how a show was put together. But someone had taken note of his fiery red hair and his mischievous laugh. He and Ronnie Clarke had managed to hook a long paper tail on a belt loop of the class president, Richard Atkins,

Sister Margaret Louise's pet, as he went about acting grown-up and responsible, asking intelligent questions.

Someone in a narrow tie asked the redhead his name and next thing he knew, he was on TV. Literally within weeks. He played a kid like himself, in fact. Shrewd producers realized what could not be written and just let him be himself. An asshole. But three-channel America loved him. The show was a hit and fame descended upon him.

Girls he had admired, who had turned up their noses at him, now spread their legs gratefully. They even sucked his dick. Just like they did in those magazines Uncle Pete had. Come to think of it, fuck Uncle Pete. He'd wanted to suck Bobby's dick, too.

It was a golden period. He was Bobby Lebow. He was sent to the Paul Heinreid cotillion at the Beverly Hilton, where he immediately won first prize. Even though he danced like an ox. In fact, he won every contest, for any aspect of talent, in which he was now entered.

Then some fool asked him if he could sing and his answer was, who couldn't! Presto! He was in a band and on the cover of *Tiger Beat*. Tiger Beat, because he, Bobby Lebow, was a tiger. Records came out, written and produced by grateful, obsequious strangers, and went gold. Or wherever they went. He was too busy to really notice.

He had a fan club. He had a fan club manager. Her job, while it lasted, for minimum wage, had been to scrawl Bobby Lebow's personal greetings and encouragements over millions of eight-by-tens.

> *Keep rockin', Bobby*
> *Keep it hard, Bobby*
> *Rock on! Bobby*
> *Rock hard, Bobby*

Then his fan club manager got pregnant. Bobby Jr. did not see the light of day. Miss Fan Club was fired, of course, but the situation was kept under control. Relative control. Management had paid out money. After all, the Bobby Lebow Train was an economic juggernaut and could not be stopped for trivial reasons.

And then, fast as a bolt of lightning, he wasn't cute anymore. Some asshole at *Rolling Stone* had reviewed his solo album, which, with one exception, he'd insisted on writing himself. The biggest part of being a genius, he'd realized, was *realizing* you were a genius. The album was a stone masterpiece, if he did say so himself.

But the ninety-pound, pimpled shit-eater at *Rolling Stone* wanted to look good for his girlfriend or something. So he dipped his pen in venom. *The worst album ever made by the most irrelevant snot-bag who's ever walked upright on planet Earth.* Who was Bobby Lebow to cover "Eleanor Rigby"?

It was a splash of ice water to the face. He looked into the mirror, into the abyss, found that every penny he'd earned had been squandered. *Squandered,* what a word. He'd blown a fortune. Plain old gone.

And then, by the will of a benevolent god, he'd had another chance. And he'd signed on, even though he'd read the script and found it beyond wretched. *Me, Dad, and Me.*

Me, Dad, and Me created the new teen sensation, Ellen Havertine. In exception to all reason, it was a big hit. A huge hit. For five years. And that money would have lasted. He'd even married Ellen. But cocaine had entered his life.

And now cocaine *was* his life. That's why he didn't live in fancy digs. As long as those residual checks came in quarterly, and Ellen's checks monthly, he could roll out to Van Nuys and score his two ounces a week, eight grams a day. Cocaine *was* his life. Though an ounce wasn't going as far these days. But now Ellen owed him fifty big ones. And had promised him a million.

He knew how he would die. After one really flawless big sweet purple hit, his heart would fail. Just stop. Maybe explode. Which was fine by him. If you're gonna do the crime, you gotta do the time. He was prepared. That's how good the shit was.

He passed Guitar Center on his right and the pierced, tattooed acolytes of Never Going to Happen.

He made a right at Sierra Bonita, drove up the street, made another right, parked on Hawthorne Avenue. What he needed was a hit.

One hit led to two, two to four. Now he was ready. He exited the car, removed a light jacket with a DHL logo. Package delivery. From the backseat he retrieved a taped-up, addressed manila envelope.

Number 1544 was one of those nice old bungalows. Pretty well taken care of. The front door was open to the nice weather. He rang the doorbell, looked through the screen door, waited.

Then the woman appeared. "Yes?"

Bobby rechecked his package. "Got a delivery for . . . for Penelope Grace?"

The woman opened the screen door. He put the envelope full of newspapers in her hand, then handed her a clipboard.

"Just sign on the open line. Where the X is."

As the woman grasped the attached pen, he made his request. "Excuse me, lady, can I use your restroom? Too much Diet Coke," he added with a pained grin.

The woman looked at him, puzzled. "Do I know you?"

Bobby smiled. With the years, he had passed into an undefined shadow fame. "I don't think so. But could I use the can?" He hopped on his right foot.

"Okay," said the lady, "in the back to the left."

"Thanks." He'd walked back there, took a relaxed piss, shook it out, studied himself in the mirror, looked through the medicine cabinet. Nothing special. He decided he'd take a quick hit. Two hits. He exited the bathroom.

The woman was right there. She looked a little put out. "You *smoking* something in there?"

"Yes," he said, smiling. Then he backhanded her across the face with all his strength, knocking her down.

In an instant he was on top of her, a knee right between her tits. "What I'm really here for is to deliver a message." He decided to slap her face. *Whack!* "You've been poking your nose places it doesn't fucking belong."

The woman raised her hand from her prone position. "I think you've made a mistake and—"

Her denial pissed him off. He grabbed her by the hair, pulled her up, slammed her head back down into the floor. Then again. And one more time. As if she were a doll. "I don't make mistakes, bitch."

She was bleeding from the mouth. A nice Technicolor crimson. "Fuck you," she said thickly.

And that did it. He went to town. Slaps turned to punches and the punches had a smooth, relaxed flow of their own. He was the Terminator.

After two or three minutes the cocaine level in his brain dropped below alpha level and he had to take a breath. Then he saw what he had done.

The woman was dead. Like a dog. Like *his* dog.

He looked at his hands. They were covered with gore and they trembled.

In the bathroom he washed face and hands. Took two hits. Three hits. Then stepped out the back door, walked around the house, out to the sidewalk.

The sounds of Sunset Boulevard, rushing traffic, bathed him in white noise. No one was looking at him. No people in the neighboring bungalows were on their porches, pointing and indignant. He walked up to Hawthorne. His gait felt normal. To question your gait meant you were walking funny already.

There was the Infiniti. He had not forgotten his keys. The car started right up, like it always did, superlative Japanese technology. He took Hawthorne to its light on La Brea. Then crossed La Brea, continued on Hawthorne, turned left after passing the back side of the Roosevelt Hotel. No red lights in his mirror. He headed up Orange, made a right into the heavy Hollywood Boulevard traffic. No lights, no guns, no nothing. Home free.

CHAPTER TWENTY-THREE

Violet Brown

Pussy Grace was in a good mood, considering. In the sack on the front seat of her 2004 Honda Accord were two roast beef sandwiches and a six-pack of Heineken from Greenblatt's. And last night she had acquired an eighth ounce of Purple Kush from Compassionate Friends, and Violet would have already rolled a fattie. It would take her mind off Art. And all that frightening shit that had gone down. It would be an afternoon of gossip and laughter. She needed a little laughter.

She parked in front of her house and went in. Something was wrong.

She stopped in her tracks. In the dining area, where she could see around the counter, the rug was pushed up and crumpled. She heard a fly buzzing.

"Violet?" The kitchen floor was splattered with redness. Redness that ran down the cabinets in streaks. *"Violet?"* Her voice had gone weak and watery. As had her knees. She tottered forward.

There was a person. A woman. Lying on her back, arms out. The face—wasn't a face anymore.

The paper bag from Greenblatt's slipped through her fingers and crashed to the ground. Beer flowed from the bag, mixing in with the redness. Who was this? C-c-could it possibly *be Violet?* Who did this? Were . . . they . . . still . . . *here?*

Her knees gave way completely and she sank down into the mess.

116

Bile came up in her throat and she retched. Flies. More flies. She crawled back the way she had come, red smears on the hardwood flooring.

The Caddy rolled west on the Sunset Strip. It was going to be a very good day.

I'd gone out to run some errands and came home to find a message from Kiyoko. I never really knew which end was up with her. Things would be going along fine and then, out of the blue, I would do something that blew the ship out of the water. Once in disgrace I was in disgrace until I wasn't. Then the sun came out from behind the clouds as if there'd never been rain.

I called her back and the day was sunny at her end. I suggested a trip to the Getty Museum. She accepted.

Any man is improved by the atmosphere of a museum. He doesn't even need to talk. In fact, it may be better if he doesn't.

All that's required is a thoughtful perusal of things he may or may not understand. Then a nod of appreciation, a chuckle of insight, the low whistle of incredulity. If you can't whistle, substitute the head shake. The side-to-sider. Stick to this regimen, exactly, and it is possible to be mistaken for a man of depth and sensitivity.

I was hoping for some Kostabi, coincidentally one of Kiyoko's favorites, but the net told me that Impressionists were currently holding sway. In fact, the current program was the contrast and comparison of Cézanne and Pissarro. With a minor in Monet and Millet. I was pretty sure Monet was Mo-*nay,* but was Millet Mill-*ay?* Or was he a common grain, millet?

Who cared? I would shut my piehole and peruse.

My cell rang. It was Kiyoko. "Hello, darling Kiyoko," I said. I was filled with a golden optimism.

"Hi, Dick. You are on the way?"

"Twenty minutes down the road."

"Hurry, Dick."

Yes, my darling. I will hurry. I heard a siren.

"What's that, Dick?" asked Kiyoko.

"It's the police."

"Are they after you?"

"They can't be. I'm as innocent as the rain. I'll talk to you later."

As soon as I hung up it rang again. Puss. I had no time for her now.

But the cops *were* after me. I crossed over from West Hollywood, entered Beverly Hills, pulled to the side. Suddenly I was surrounded and guns were in my face.

"Get out of the car, asshole. Real slow. And keep those hands where I can see 'em."

I tried to be a nice guy in the middle of a big mistake but the guys were dead serious and weren't buying. I was handcuffed, dragged to the rat wagon, taken to the Beverly Hills lockup.

I hadn't been there since all the shit went down with Artie Benjamin. The place hadn't improved.

No doubt this was part of the Art Lewis caper. Which would be why Pussy had tried to call me. They jacked her up, got her talking, and she started spilling beans. Even imaginary beans. Then she'd loyally called to warn me. Or, loyal to the police, called to lure me in. I tried to get my thoughts in order.

Art Lewis was dead. Or I had seen him die. I had nothing to do with it. But I had known about it and had done nothing. *Conspiracy after the fact.*

Art was dead. Or I had seen him die. Then I had seen Puss knock out Nursie with a cane. I had done nothing and run away. *Conspiracy after the fact, flight to avoid.*

I had stolen a Gas Company van, impersonated a Gas Company

employee. Art was dead or I had seen him die. I allowed or directed Puss to assault Nursie. Then I split. *Theft, impersonation, assault, conspiracy, flight to avoid.*

I'd stolen the van. I'd impersonated personnel. I told Pussy to attack the nurse. I watched Art die. Then I split. Then I engineered a wedding with a dead groom. With plans to drain his bank accounts. *Theft, impersonation, assault, depraved indifference, flight to avoid, conspiracy, fiscal and marital malfeasance.* Then, surely, they would add the sinister, Orwellian condition my music-business friend, Tom Sturges, a nonlawyer, had concocted: third-party prior knowledge of fact.

In other words, I was fucked. No. In those very words. *Theft, impersonation, assault, depraved indifference, flight to avoid, conspiracy, fiscal and marital malfeasance, third-party prior.*

I was cooked. An apple in my mouth.

Well, I had my one phone call coming. I'd be calling Andy Rigrod.

I was taken to an interrogation room. It was cold and bright, and I sat there thinking of Kiyoko. Certainly, this was the final end.

The door opened and someone walked in. I knew him by the sound of his shoes. It would be Lew Peedner, my former friend and partner. I looked over. Lieutenant Ferguson was with him.

He sat at the other end of the table. He looked at me, shook his head. "Here we are again, Dick."

I said nothing.

The science of interrogation is based on the fact that bullshit, ordinary or purposeful, eventually reveals facts and attitudes of the speaker. Just get the guy to talk. And keep him talking. Eventually he'll hang himself.

High in the ceiling, cameras were recording the interview.

"Here we are again, Dick," Peedner repeated. "In another big pile of shit."

Again, I said nothing.

"So, where do you fit in, Dick?"

I shrugged.

"You have no idea why you're here?"

"I was dragged here."

"Another sheer coincidence."

I shrugged again.

"This time, Dick, I think I've got you dead to rights."

"Then you better read me my rights, Lew."

Lew's life had been hell since I'd punched Elton Reese's ticket. He'd never forgiven me. And had the situation been reversed, I doubted if I could have forgiven him. Though Elton Reese, child killer, richly deserved to die, he was not a white man and his genetic inheritance became the center of the matter.

"Read Mr. Henry his rights, Lieutenant."

Ferguson set in. "You have the right to remain silent. Anything you say can and will be used against you in a court of law. You have the right to speak to an attorney and have an attorney present during questioning. If you cannot afford an attorney, one will be provided at government expense. Have I made myself clear, Mr. Henry?"

What a country. In my mind I could see Lewis stone dead, could feel that CPR perspiration rolling down my back.

"Knowing and understanding your rights as I have explained them, do you wish to talk to us at this time?"

I saw Pussy step from the shadows and whack Nursie across the head.

You should never, ever talk to the police, but I wanted to know where they were coming from. I could always clam up and call Rigrod.

"Let's talk," I said.

Ferguson broke out paper and pen. Lew Peedner stared at me. "When was the last time you saw Pussy Grace?"

"Couple of days ago." *It's called spontaneous combustion, Dick.*

"Where were you?"

"Third and Fairfax, Farmers Market."

"When was the last time you were at her house?"

"I don't know. A week? A week ago?"

"Where were you between twelve-forty-five and one-thirty this afternoon?"

This afternoon. The image of dead Art and unconscious Nursie fell to pieces in my mind. "Today? Where was I between twelve-forty-five and one-thirty today?"

"Where were you?"

"At my house. Laurel Canyon."

"Were you with anybody?"

"No."

"Nobody?"

"No. Wait. The mail lady delivered. I talked to her."

Peedner and Ferguson looked at one another.

"Will you submit to a luminol test?" asked Ferguson.

"Bring it on." *Had something happened to Puss?*

Lew held up a plastic baggie. "Know what this is?"

It looked like a Zippo lighter. "Looks like a Zippo."

"It has your name on it, Dick. 'To Dick, love always, G.'"

"That's mine. Where'd you find it?"

"At the murder scene."

I shot to my feet. "Puss? No!"

Peedner shook his head. "Pussy's alright. You know Violet Brown?"

I had a sick feeling in my gut. "Of course, I do. Friend of Puss. Girlfriend of a friend. Is she—"

"She was murdered this afternoon. At Pussy's."

My mind spun through the possibilities.

Peedner honed right in with the instincts that made him such a good cop. "Do you think Violet Brown was the intended victim of this crime?"

"I don't know."

"Do you know if Violet Brown was *not* the intended victim of this crime?"

"I don't know that, either."

"What do you know?" I could feel his eyes on me. "You know something."

I shrugged, spread my hands.

"You're not planning to leave town anytime soon, are you Dick?"

"Nowhere to go." Which was the sad truth.

I looked up at Lew. "How ya been, Lew?"

"I've been, Dick."

CHAPTER TWENTY-FOUR

You Like Animals?

An hour and half after the luminol came back negative I was released. Puss was in the lobby. She looked like hell. She rushed into my arms and I held her.

Puss gave me a ride, so I could get the Caddy out of impound on Fuller. The impound-lot secretary was a little surly. I was only trying to be friendly with the old battleax, but her humor had leaked out a long time ago.

"You look better every time I come to visit," I said cheerfully.

"Oh, yeah?" she rasped, sucking on a Lucky Strike, then stabbing it out. "Maybe you should try not to get your vehicle impounded so often."

"I only get my car impounded when I get accused of murder," I pointed out coldly.

My comment did nothing for her disposition. But it did make her shut up and think.

As I waited for the Caddy to be released, I called Doc Peach.

He sounded relaxed. Which meant his office was stuffed with blue-haired ladies, blue poodles, and the occasional little girl, blue, with her overfed hamster. Her *blue* hamster. "Can I do something for you, Dick?" asked Peach.

I told him. How a friend of mine, Penelope Grafton, had come home to find a murder scene. I wondered if he still had the little apartment above the clinic?

Yes, he did. And it was empty, basically. Boxes of records. He was eager to help. "Any friend of yours is a friend of mine. Bring her right over."

Three scenarios.

First, a grudge killing. Violet, in the photos I'd been shown, looked like she'd been beaten by someone who hated her. But who knew she was at Puss's place?

Second. Mistaken identity. The killer had come for Puss, found Violet, didn't know the difference. But why the unmerciful beating, why the unprofessional rage?

Third. Some evil, boulevard dope fiend wandered into Puss's by chance, attacked and killed Violet for spare change and carry-away junk. Remember to ask Puss if anything was missing.

There wasn't a fourth scenario. But all the same I wondered. Was this connected to Art Lewis?

Twenty-five minutes later Puss and I arrived at Abbot Kinney, parked behind the building. Clark came out to meet her. I don't know what he expected. Well, yes I do. He expected Penelope Grafton. A thickly spectacled librarian with a mortuary tan, no figure, bad posture, and bad skin. Instead, he met Pussy Grace.

Pussy, on her worst day, which this may have been, was a seven-sector call-out, a thionite dream. Even shrouded in shock and sorrow, her feminine radiance could not be concealed.

"Dr. Peach," I said gravely, "this is Miss Penelope Grafton. Penelope, this is Dr. Peach."

"How do you do, P-penelope?" Doc Peach was staggered. He put out his hand, Puss took it. Dick Henry had entirely disappeared from his mind.

"Thank you, Doctor," said Puss quietly. "I won't be a bother."

The doc quickly recovered his sea legs. "A bother? How would that be possible? No bother at all."

He turned to me, recalling I had been in the vicinity. "Just leave her with me. Maybe she can help me out around here a little bit."

He turned to Puss. "What do you say? You like animals?"

I left the clinic, walked to Electric Avenue, found Dennis Donnelly's house. I called first. "Just wanted to stop by a second."

I could tell by his voice he already was lost in what had gone down. "Come in, dude," he said.

Dennis was drinking and smoking but it was no use. Wherever he turned, she wasn't. I said all the right things. All of them ridiculous and stupid. Finally, mercifully, he nodded out. I laid him back on his couch, covered him with a blanket.

CHAPTER TWENTY-FIVE

Recriminations

From the kitchen window Harry could see the waves rush onto the shore. He'd figured it out. One hundred seventeen feet of waterfront, for which he paid $7 million, meant he'd paid $59,829 per foot. How many times had he actually walked the beach? Maybe ten. Six of those in the first two weeks. Now the place was killing him.

He and Ellen were having a light meal. Salads and BLTs on sourdough. But still he felt queasy.

He had never felt quite so unsettled, so off-balance, in his life. For chrissake, he, Judge Harold J. Glidden, was involved in a *criminal conspiracy*. He didn't understand how real criminals did this. Lived with the doubts, the fears, much less the recriminations. Maybe they didn't recriminate. Because they were criminals. Harold J. Glidden couldn't help it.

Ellen's nonchalance bewildered him. He looked across the table. What had he been thinking? He didn't know this woman. *Marry in haste, repent at leisure*. But he couldn't have done that. He was Harold J. Glidden.

Yet right this second, *right this second,* Art Lewis, stiff as a country ham, lay in his own walk-in freezer. Surrounded by steaks and chops and vegetables that would never be eaten. Frost would be slowly accumulating in his ears, in his nostrils.

And the marriage! He'd performed a marriage for a dead man. Of course they'd hadn't bothered to pretend. But, alibi in mind, they'd joyfully bought a thousand dollars' worth of champagne from Jerry's Liquor Barn and left Jerry a huge tip for luck. Jerry could testify to their happiness. Eileen, married at last!

Eileen was not only dull, deadly dull, she was the cause of dullness in others. Art Lewis, in a million years, would never have married her. He would have married the maid first. Or even the gardener.

Ellen swallowed a forkful of arugula with honey mustard. Harry was worrying again. What was the good of worrying? The dice had been cast and things would happen as they were meant to occur. God helped those who helped themselves. And that's what they were doing. Helping themselves. Before the ESP/UFO/reincarnation phonies helped themselves. Why should those charlatans rake it in?

She needed a smoke. "What's wrong, Harry? There a bug in your salad?"

"Bill Archibald asked me about the wedding today."

"What did you say?"

"That it was touching."

Instinct told her he'd hadn't stopped there. "What else did you say?"

"Nothing."

"What kind of nothing?"

"I said how much Art seemed to love Eileen."

Ellen shook her head. "You just can't shut up. I'm going to puke."

"Bill seemed to think it was a little sudden."

"It was sudden, Harold. He was dead."

The judge drained his wine. "I keep running into his friends, for chrissake. I didn't know he had so many."

She lit up. "Well, just shut up. That's all you have to do." She turned on the TV. "They're just pissed you were invited and they weren't."

She unmuted the set as the cameras pushed in on Clark Kent's brother, Ted Sargent. "Good evening, everyone, I'm Ted Sargent," said Ted Sargent. Ted was as earnest as a brake shoe and just as smart.

"Welcome to the ten o'clock news. Our top story tonight—a gruesome murder in Hollywood."

Six cop cars, lights flashing, came up on screen. Ellen recognized an older section of Tinseltown. Square-jaw continued, "This afternoon police were summoned to 1544 North Sierra Bonita Avenue, where the body of a woman was found."

Ellen felt a rush of sickness. *It couldn't be.* Please say it *isn't.*

"The victim, a woman in her thirties, whose name is being withheld, was savagely beaten and died at the scene. The police, commenting unofficially on the severity of her injuries, said her condition was quote *grotesquely sickening* unquote. Now, on a lighter note, today in Brentwood, a bear—"

Ellen snapped it off. It was hard to breathe. Her husband looked up at her.

"You alright?"

Ellen nodded, not speaking. "I'm going shopping."

"Shopping? At this hour? For what?"

"Feminine products, Harry. Want to come with me?"

She walked out.

He heard the garage door go up. Then go down. Who *was* she? She was going *shopping?*

A shameful word occurred to him. With it came a churning in his gut. *Cuckold.* Was he, a man who'd labored honestly his entire life, now a pitiful cuckold?

He remembered the first time they'd made love. In Newport. Good God. She knew things. She knew a lot of things. And she did them. Went boldly where no man had gone before. He corrected himself. Where no *woman* had gone before. Men—out of the question.

Was she now flying to the arms of a lover?

He threw the salad bowl across the room, where it shattered.

Cuckold.

Cuckold.

Bobby had just cooked up a few big boogers when he heard her knock on the door. The knocks came fast. She was pissed. He'd heard her trying to control herself on her cell phone, which was, in effect, public broadcasting.

"Who is it?" he sang sweetly.

"It's me, you asshole, open up." A hissing whisper.

Ahh. His former child bride. Maybe he'd let her wait, fix himself a purple hit. Naaah. He'd wait for the hit. And anticipate.

He opened the door and she was in, throwing her purse to the floor.

"Do you realize what the fuck you've done?"

"What have I done?"

"You were going to *talk* to that woman."

"I did. What's the problem?"

Was it possible he didn't know? "You killed her, Bobby. *You killed her.* You stupid piece of shit. It's all over the news. You beat her to death."

Bobby shook his head, absolutely sure. "I didn't do that. I didn't do that." He applied his Bic to the loaded liquor spout. He heard the tiny crackling, heralding that purple vapor. And . . . and there was the *rrrrush.* He set the pipe down, looked at Ellen, shook his head again. "I didn't kill anybody. No fuckin' way. No way."

He fixed two pipes, slid one across the coffee table. She picked it up automatically.

The woman was dead. There was nothing she could do about that.

She hadn't wanted it. She hadn't ordered it. Had certainly taken no pleasure in it. Maybe the woman was with Art in paradise.

Strippers would be welcomed in heaven. Of course they would. Cousins of Mary Magdalene. Lots of wine would be served. They'd make it from water. From the clouds. They'd wash some feet, too.

Maybe Bobby hadn't done it. Maybe he hadn't. He said he didn't.

But accidentally, purely accidentally, the killing had served a purpose. A witness was mute.

The only loose end was doofus Dick-Dave. He'd be at the woman's funeral, no doubt. And then he could be taken care of. One way or the other.

She applied a flame. *Ohhhh, yessss.*

CHAPTER TWENTY-SIX

A Visit to Myron Ealing

I rolled down Hollywood Boulevard toward the Hollywood Professional Building, the southwest corner of Hollywood and Cahuenga.

I had talked to Puss last night. She was doing well at Doc Peach's. She'd shampooed a collie, which, apparently, was as hard as it got as far as dogs were concerned. Fine hair. I'd asked her if she'd ever given Ellen Havertine her address. After the dinner with Art, maybe?

No, she said, but then she changed her mind. "Actually, I did. We were talking about classical dance and she said she'd send me some tapes of Dame Fonteyn."

"I think I've heard of her," I said.

"Sounds like a country-western singer," said Puss. "I thought she was going to send me classical dance tapes. Whatever."

"What else went on? At the dinner? Anything else?"

"Nothing," said Puss, "just dinner."

But that put Puss's address in the hands of the marriage brokers. I decided I needed to know as much as I could about Ellen Havertine.

So I parked across from World Book & News, waved at Smilin' Jack Hathaway, went up to see Myron Ealing.

How a man lived on a diet of stale popcorn and Diet Dr. Pepper I couldn't imagine. Myron weighed somewhere over four hundred pounds but over short distances he was extremely fast. As various adversaries could ruefully attest.

A failed mathematician, Myron had a mind like a steel trap— a trap that had rusted out on the liquid minutiae of string theory. There were eleven dimensions but five through eleven were tiny and in Einstein's pants but the pants were at a Chinese laundry and the laundry was closed.

No tickee, no washee.

Temporarily stymied, Myron decided he would compile the Encyclopedia of Pornography, and that research led directly into the sleazy white underbelly of Hollywood. Now he had the dirt on anyone who had gotten dirty. And who hadn't?

"Ellen Havertine," I said. "What do you know?"

Myron dug into his barrel of Christmas corn. Half-price if purchased in January. Of lasting freshness. "I know everything."

"Let's have it."

Myron leaned back, closed his eyes, set his prodigious mind to work. "Precocious child actor at nine. Caught smoking pot on the set at eleven."

I felt a faint tickle of memory.

Myron opened his eyes. "Remember Dick Shale?"

"No."

"TV director. Episodic. *Hill St. Blues, Houston,* some pilots. The breed wasn't as well respected then."

I shrugged. "Never heard of him."

"Well, at fourteen she seduces him—"

"You mean, he seduced her."

"No. She came into his office, sat in his lap, sucked his cock. Then blackmailed him."

"When an adult has sex with a child it's the adult's fault."

Ealing raised a meaty hand. "I agree. The fault was his. I'm just saying she wasn't the ordinary, pigtailed fourteen-year-old.

She knew things and used them. Where she learned them, I don't know."

Ealing brought up a new page on his computer. "Anyhow, she got him to put her up for *Me, Dad, and Me,* and the rest is history. They made the pilot into a show and by fifteen she was a network star. Two hundred grand a week. Age nineteen, three seventy-five a week, she marries one of her costars. Bobby Lebow. Lebow was twenty-three."

"I remember him. Redhead. Curly hair, played guitar. Teen magazines and stuff."

"A *Tiger Beat* heartthrob. He acted, well, he acted like himself, he played a little guitar, had a couple of hits, he did a few chop-socky flicks. But then he grew up, was headed straight for the pimple heap. *Me, Dad, and Me* saved his ass. Then, like everything else in the world, *Me, Dad, and Me* was canceled and he'd worn out his welcome and did a quick fade. Still lives here in Hollywood."

"Where's Tarantino when you need him?"

"No shit. And, boy, does he ever. If rumor holds true, he lives right up here on Cherokee."

"Whitley Heights?"

"Not that far up. The Cherokee Hotel. Not far from the Blackstone, Playboy Liquor."

"That's junkie territory."

"I hear he's into coke. But maybe not. He was a pro rehabber for a while."

"That didn't last?"

"I don't think so. You got to be humble, naturally humble. That's not Bobby."

"Back to Ellen, please."

"Let's see. Her marriage to Bobby fucked up the show. But she went on, made a couple of things, flamed out on the big screen. Then she married a director, Gus Tchamtik."

"Better than marrying a writer."

"She and Gus had a nice little run, he did a Sharon Stone thing, but in the end she squeezed him dry and dropped him. Then she met Judge Glidden on the set of *Law & Order*. Pretty soon the good judge kicked his wife of twenty-seven years to the curb."

"Bye-bye, Patricia."

"I think her name was Marcia."

"No. It's Patricia."

"Which liar told you that?"

"The judge himself."

Myron put his head back and laughed.

CHAPTER TWENTY-SEVEN

Indian Dinner Theater

Of course Ellen had never given her the $25,000 she'd promised. And now here she was in the middle of nowhere, the middle of the desert, on her "honeymoon," marooned at an Indian casino. Fucking marooned. How many manicures and pedicures did a person really need?

And then she'd been Jacuzzied, shrimp-cocktailed, Bloody Mary'd, and massaged with special Indian mud. Was that chick trying to hit on her? She wasn't sure, so she let it pass. Maybe Indians liked lots of mud on their tits.

Then she'd sat through the Indian Heritage Dance Review, but it had been done better at Disneyland. DUM-dum-dum-dum DUM-dum-dum-dum, those fucking drums. She was dead sure that she recognized one of the drummers, the one with the fucked-up feathers. He was one of the lunchtime busboys at Cielo Lindo, the upscale restaurant place where a significant portion of the fresh Native Salmon Feast had still been frozen. She'd almost broken a tooth. The only thing she'd managed to avoid was Indian Dinner Theater. But she wouldn't be able to hold out much longer. DUM-dum-dum-dum DUM-dum-dum-dum. *Jesus.*

Honeymoon. What a joke. The big dead cocksucker must have weighed three hundred pounds. There was no gurney. Nothing professional. Of course. So they'd wrapped him in a rug and dragged his dead ass feet first down the stairs. If he wasn't dead yet, that did it. His head banging every step on the way down.

Then arguing with that smart-ass cokehead who used to be her brother-in-law. A long time ago she'd thought he was funny but now, God, she loathed him. She half-remembered him coming into her room one night when Ellen was away and making her feel him. She must have been fifteen. But maybe that didn't happen.

Fuck it.

Medically speaking, he was going to kill himself with cocaine. And that would be fine by her.

CHAPTER TWENTY-EIGHT

Truths Laid Bare

The service was at St. Paul of Tarsus in Hollywood. There's not a single good thing about a funeral. No matter how cheap, they're expensive; no matter the pomp, they're meaningless; and not a single attendee, living or dead, with the exception of mortuary personnel, wants to be there. It was no different with the funeral of Violet Brown.

At the rear of the church, representing O'Halloran's, was Billy Ravenich, my friend from Navy days. Billy owned seven black suits. All of them write-offs. He attended up to fifteen funerals a week, depending on traffic. After long practice, his performance had moved beyond words. Now he clapped those who would be comforted on the shoulder and nodded silently, slowly, looking into their eyes. What did words mean, after all? Few noticed the tiny wire and earpiece. Dodgers, Kings, Lakers. Me, I miss Chick Hearn and the popcorn machine.

I walked toward the back, stood with Billy. He put a hand on my shoulder and nodded. I nodded back.

I was there for Dennis, spiritually, for Puss, physically. Things were going swell down at Doc Peach's but I wondered who might show up at the service.

Prudently assuming the worst, Violet's demise had been meant for Puss. Meaning someone had fingered her. It couldn't have been the nurse. She hadn't seen that much of Puss before Puss had caned her. Which probably meant a security system. If so, Puss and I were on video. But Puss could have been identified only by someone who knew her. And that someone would have to have knowledge of Art's security system. Everything went back to Puss's dinner with Judge Glidden and Ellen Havertine. Where Puss had given Havertine her address. And had shown her Art's security system.

"You showed her Art's security system? I thought you said nothing happened that night."

"Nothing did," said Puss, oblivious. "Art just asked me to show her around."

"And you showed her the security system."

"I showed her the walk-in freezers, too."

Yes, Ellen Havertine's prints were all over this thing. And if her companions wanted to kill Puss, certainly I was next on the list.

Reverend Jenkins walked out of the sacristy and the service began. The reverend, now in his seventy-second year, was a true foot soldier of Christ and had worked long hours in the vineyard of lost souls. We were friends of a sort.

Prayers came and went and then it got personal. He turned to the twenty or so mourners and spoke to the Creator on behalf of all.

"Father, we ask you to accept the spirit of Violet Patrice into Your Presence, to forgive her sins, to comfort her, to hold her close to Thee. We also ask that You comfort those she left behind, reminding them that life is eternal in Jesus Christ. Reminding them that all love sundered in this world will find a day restored. We ask these things in the name of the Lord."

"Amen," said Dennis Donnelly, gently but deeply drunk. He swayed in place, tears streaming down his cheeks.

I couldn't imagine what he would do without Violet. They'd each been through a lot, lost their hearts in fruitless chasings, renounced love as a conjurer's deceit, then, stony-eyed and skeptical, found each other. They settled into a solid rhythm around their own sun, oblivious to all others. They had their vices, transparent to both, they took their pleasures. It was a lifetime groove, *on 'Lectric Aven-oo,* you could see it.

But goodbye to all that.

Behind me a measured, authoritative pair of high heels entered the church, approached. A scarfed woman put her hand on Billy's arm. "Excuse me," she said in a low voice, peering toward the altar, "this is the service for Violet Brown, isn't it?"

I turned, looked across Billy at Ellen Havertine. An evil joy filled me as speculations turned to probabilities. "Ellen Havertine?" I inquired.

She turned, her eyes went wide. "You!"

"Yeah, me." She knew me. She'd seen videotape. "But what are *you* doing here, Ms. Havertine?"

Then Puss walked up, eyes swollen, recognized Ellen, goggled. "What are you doing here?"

Ellen whirled to Puss, jaw dropping to her chest. Then she turned and ran out of the church.

Puss looked at me. "What's her problem?"

I grinned a cold grin. Certain things were clear to me now. "She thought you were dead."

Havertine had just settled into her yellow Mercedes when I hustled up. I tapped on her window. She started the car, lowered the window three inches.

I pointed at her. "I know who you are. And I know what you've done. And I'm going to fuck up your party big-time. You're not going to get a goddamn penny and your ass is going to rot in jail."

She flipped me the bird, put the window up. I pointed at the beautiful murderess, drew my finger across my throat, turned, walked for the Caddy.

If I'd been postulating before, now I knew. Ellen Havertine and Hangin' Harry were the opposition.

I heard a squeal of tires. I turned, dived onto my belly as the Mercedes, coming backwards, shrieked to a stop. The passenger's window came down, she leaned across the seat, looked down at me on the pavement. "Don't worry about my ass, Dick-Dave, I know how to take care of it. Now smile for me." She held up her cell phone, snapped my picture.

Before I caught my breath she shoved the Mercedes into gear, banged out of the parking lot, turned up toward Franklin, floored it, left rubber.

And to think, she'd been *People* magazine's Sweetest Girl in the World two years running.

But my heart had turned cold. Violet Brown's blood and Dennis Donnelly's tears made it personal. *Very personal.* Like Sun Tzu said in the *Art of War,* some battles are not meant to be fought.

But some are.

I stood up, brushed off the little stones imbedded in my palms. Puss finally arrived on scene. "Jesus. She doesn't know how to drive."

Pure Puss. Homing in on the essentials.

"Go back to Venice, Puss."

"Who's Dick-Dave, Dick?"

Oh, shut up. Dick-Dave-Dick.

What would Ellen Havertine do with my picture? It didn't really matter. I knew my adversaries.

Woe unto them.

CHAPTER TWENTY-NINE

You Pay Him

East on Hollywood Boulevard. Stupid, stupid, *stupid*. Inquiring, unofficially, about the murder on Sierra Bonita Avenue, Harry's secretary, Arnelle, had given her the name Violet Brown. Then, foolishly, Ellen had assumed Pussy Grace was a stage name—for Violet Brown. Glaringly, at the church, she'd revealed her ignorance to Dick-Dave. Her obvious surprise at seeing Pussy Grace alive and well, 36 double-D. She would kill Bobby. *Kill* him.

And Dick-Dave didn't put out a gofer vibration. He was dangerous. Who was he? She'd find out. She had his photograph.

She parked behind Musso & Frank's. She wondered if the three valet Mexicans in the greasy red jackets lived in that kiosk. They watched her come over for a ticket, started laughing among themselves.

She could tell the subject across the lot. What else? Pussy. Well, she still had it, baby, breakin' out all over. And all men, real men, were fools for it. She snapped the ticket out of the ringleader's fingers. She could hear them giggling as she stalked away. Grown men.

Her mother. Vicious, disappointed, cynical, alcoholic. The things Ellen had learned at her knee. At her elbow. *In her bed.*

After Jack, her husband, had disappeared, Agnetha Havertine had entertained a series of men. Ellen would meet them in the afternoon, at the kitchen table, after she came home from school. The visitor and mom would be drinking and smoking. Laughing.

What happened to Daddy, she'd asked one day. A day of no visitors.

Her mom laughed but her laugh was inside-out. You want to know the truth, Ellen? You want to know the *truth*?

I guess so.

Well, yes or no?

I *guess* so.

Well, I'll tell you. I mean, look at you. You're starting to grow yourself a chest. You should know.

Men wanted one thing. They wanted to fuck. As long as testosterone flowed through their bodies, that's all they wanted. Every act they committed, public or private, great or small, conscious or unconscious, was in furtherance of the overwhelming, unquenchable, unswerving drive to *fuck*.

Now, some men did everything but the final step—the actual fucking—but, still, their every action was motivated by the exact same desire. Those who had forsworn the act itself basked in the knowledge that their demonstrations of intelligence, daring, and courage allowed them the rarest of pleasures. They would cultivate a woman's hunger, then walk nobly away from it. Possessing her in the negative.

Men were all the same.

Then that night. That night she had been unable to sleep and, dressed in her pajamas, had knocked softly and entered her mother's room. The room was dim. And it smelled. Then she saw there was a man in the bed.

Looking back, Ellen could not remember the little girl she had been. Was absolutely unable to recall her feelings, her inclinations. As for desires, she couldn't have had any. Can one desire what one can't imagine?

But that night, she lay in the near dark between her mom and the man. Ellen withdrew her mind from the memories.

What did that make Mom? Didn't matter now. Her aortic artery had burst. Rest in peace, Mom. If you can.

But when the time came to deal with that prick producer, Dick Shale, little Ellen Havertine had known how.

Ellen reached the glory that was the Cherokee Hotel and climbed to the third floor.

As soon as Bobby opened the door she started in. "I just came from church, asshole. You not only fucking killed someone, you killed the wrong someone. Guess who I just met? Fucking Pussy Grace prancing down the aisle. With her partner, Dick-Dave."

"She was prancing?" Bobby flicked his Bic.

"Bobby, you killed a woman named Violet. Probably the stripper's friend."

He set the pipe down, stared at her. "I didn't kill anyone. *Bitch*. I would know if I killed someone. Because *I* would have done it. So don't walk in here on your high horse. People die all over town, every fuckin' day. Accidental falls, car accidents, electrocutions, poison. It's the luck of the draw. Wrong place, wrong time, your ticket gets punched. I didn't kill anyone."

"Alright, Bobby."

"Good. That's settled. Want a hit?"

"First this." She held her phone across the table. "This was the guy at the house. I saw him at church. He knows me now."

Bobby looked, relaxed, packed pipes. "That guy? Don't worry. He already knew you. And I know *him*."

"Who is he?"

"That's Dick Henry."

"Dick Henry."

Bobby laughed. "This's the guy you thought was a rube?"

"Who is he?"

"That's the Shortcut Man, baby. The fixer. Everybody knows Dick Henry." He lit up. "Everyone but you, you idiot."

"He said he was going to fuck me up."

Bobby nods. "And he will—if you let him."

"How do I stop him?"

Bobby rubs thumb and forefinger together. "You pay him."

"Then he can be dealt with."

He slid a pipe across the table. "Everyone's got a price."

Ellen picked up the pipe. Soon she would taste that fragrant purpleness. Wouldn't care about a goddamn thing. And this ugly, fetid little hotel room in this shitty part of Hollywood would be transformed into a companionable way station along the road of life.

All promises of the pipe were false, of course. Lies from the father of lies. But she knew that. She knew that. That was the difference. Between her, the falling, and the fallen.

She heard that tiny, rustling combustion and then the purple vapor was drawn down her throat. Her heartbeat stepped up a notch, her mentality pressurized behind her eyes, and the yellow bulb on the wire went gold.

CHAPTER THIRTY

Rutland Returns

The phone rang at 8:39 a.m. It had to be a stranger. I picked up. "What."

"Is this Mr. Dick Henry?"

"Possibly. Who's this?"

"This is Rutland. Rutland Atwater."

Rutland . . . *ahh.* Rutland, the library stinker. I hadn't heard from Mrs. Dunlap again. Maybe this was the first salvo in a bodily-injury beef.

"What do you want?"

"I want to meet with you."

"Why?"

"I think we could do business."

"I'm not susceptible to blackmail, Rutland. Get fucked."

I hung up. I had been enjoying a nice dream. Now just tatters remained, disconnected and wispy. The sky had been green and I'd been breathing underwater. I decided to make coffee.

The phone rang again.

"Dick, it's Rutland."

"I thought I told you to get fucked."

"You did."

"But you haven't?"

"I have a business proposition."

"I don't see how we could do business."

"I do. We can meet at a park and my spiel will last less than two minutes. Two minutes is all I ask."

At the park. Well, he knew part of what I was thinking. "You're serious?"

"Dead serious, Dick."

Business came from strange places. "Okay, Rutland. Plummer Park. By the basketball court. Ten o'clock."

"See you there."

In my youth, Plummer Park had been a nice little neighborhood hang. Some old relics playing checkers, babies in the sandbox, kids on swings, a lonesome few playing tennis in their little white suits.

Later, with perestroika, the Russian Empire collapsed and half the population, seemingly, migrated to West Hollywood and took over Plummer Park. Lock, stock, and balalaika.

They overwhelmed the picnic tables and everything else, leaning on canes, glowering and overweight. Nothing could rouse them from mordant preoccupation with the past. What we needed around here was a dictator issuing orders to dance.

Which reminded me. How do you get a bear to ride a unicycle?

Nail his feet to the pedals and beat the shit out of him.

I entered on Vista Street, walked toward the basketball courts. Ahead of me I saw Rutland moving into the picnic table area. The tables were full. Except for a single place at the end of the table nearest the court. Rutland waved at the immigrants in friendly fashion and sat down.

I figured I was about sixty seconds behind him. But before I arrived, as if by magic, the table cleared. Completely. The refugees looking back in alarm and disgust, gesticulating. *Holding their noses.*

So that's how you get Russians out of Plummer Park. I approached, waved to Rutland, sat upwind.

"Hi, Dick," said Rutland Atwater, force of nature, conqueror of Kiev.

I looked at my watch, held up two fingers. "You got two minutes, Rutland. Let's hear what you got to say."

Rutland folded his hands, looked at me. "I googled you."

"Yeah?"

"You're the guy who plugged Elton Reese."

We were getting off to a bad start. "That's right."

"They call you the Shortcut Man." The big man relaxed a little bit. "Our encounter at the library. It made me think. I don't want to continue living like I have been."

Did he want a recommendation to the Boy Scouts?

"I want to make money. I want to drive a Mercedes. I want a nice apartment. I want to smoke good medical marijuana. I want to fuck beautiful women."

Ambition.

I didn't exactly see where this was going but I was surprised.

"And I owe it all to you." Rutland smiled.

"You have to find women without olfactory glands."

Rutland laughed, slapped his knee. "And they're out there, Dick, they're out there. They've got to be." He rubbed thumb and forefinger together. "And maybe I'll even take a bath. Though I can't tell the difference."

"Where are you going to get money?"

Rutland smiled affably. "From you, Dick. You're going to give it to me." He raised a finger. "Not blackmail. Not by any means. You won't *give* me anything. But you'll pay me. And you'll pay me well."

I was intrigued. "What is it that you do better than anyone else, may I ask?"

Rutland clapped his huge, fat hands. "I stink, Dick. That's what I do. I stink. To high heaven. And beyond."

He gestured at the Russians. "Did you see them? Running like sheep. The lions of Leningrad! I communicate flawlessly, right across any language barrier. And that's how I'm going to work for you. When you need someone to pay up, to do what you want, and they resist, they have other ideas? Fine. You send *me* to their office, to their reception room. And I sit there, reading magazines, scratching my fat ass, until they pay up." Rutland grinned from ear to filthy ear. "And they'll pay quick." He shrugged. "I got lemons, I'm making lemonade. How can I fail?"

I spread my hands. It might work. "Rutland, you could be a genius." There was something I liked about this guy. As long as I didn't inhale.

Rutland nodded, smiled.

That's how the Shortcut Man and Rutland Atwater commenced business.

CHAPTER THIRTY-ONE

A Man of Value

It was my fourth call to Perlman, Toothaker, and Westmoreland.

"Perlman, Toothaker, and Westmoreland," said the receptionist.

"Bob Bateman, please," I intoned. I imagined myself wearing a starched white shirt, a silk tie, double-worsted wool trousers, whatever that meant, and a pair of thin-soled, tasseled Italian loafers.

A new voice came on the line, smooth and haughty. "Robert Bateman's office."

Kathryn Holler spent twenty-seven minutes on her hair every morning and did her makeup in the car on the way downtown to work for a raging psychopath.

"Bob, please."

"May I ask who's calling?"

"This is Dick Henry."

"And the nature of your call?"

"Big Bob owes money."

A pause.

"Hold on, please."

Bateman looked up from his desk to see Kathryn in the doorway. "What?" he barked. The Weatherford matter had driven him certifiably insane.

"I'm sorry, Mr. Bateman. You have a call on line three."

"From whom?"

"Dick Henry." Putting up with Screaming Bob Bateman was not worth twelve hundred dollars a week. But she had her bills to pay. "He wants money," she added, unnecessarily. Just to see that vein on his asshole forehead.

"Goddamnit," screamed Bob, punching up line three. "I thought I told you never to call here again, Mr. Henry. What don't you understand?"

"Mr. Bateman. You owe my client a sum of money. I'm wondering if I could expect your remittance today in the form of a cashier's check."

"Fuck if I'll pay a penny."

"Are you sure?"

"Fuck if I'll pay a penny."

"I'm guessing you don't want to pay."

"Fuck if I'll pay a penny."

"Fine, Bob. I'm going to send my associate, Mr. Rutland Atwater, over to your office. I've instructed him to wait until the full remittance is made."

"Fuck if I'll pay a penny."

"Thank you for your time, Mr. Bateman."

Bateman, triumphant, slammed down the phone. You don't fuck with Bob Bateman.

At ten-forty-five the wide cherrywood door of Perlman, Toothaker, and Westmoreland opened to admit a large gentleman with an alligator briefcase.

Polly, the receptionist, looked up at the man advancing toward her and gave him her professional smile of greeting. But by the time the man arrived at her desk, she had become aware of a vast, sickening odor, a miasma that attacked her eyes, her nose, and seemingly penetrated her skin. God, if she didn't know better, she was going to—

She dived for the trash can and violently unloaded the Ramona's Cheese Burrito she had unwisely scarfed at ten-fifteen.

From her knees, she looked up at the man. He was smiling. Was it possible he smelled nothing? She thought of recent headaches Dr. Vuong had dismissed. Doctors! Fools all. She was dying. An olfactory tumor. Metastasizing in her head. A grape going onion.

She staggered to her feet. "Excuse me," she said. "I think I have a tumor. Can I help you?"

"I'm here to see Bob Bateman."

"Do you have an appoin—" Another wave of sickness rolled over her, she went down again, retched into the can.

At that moment Mrs. Holiday, the office manager, walked into the reception area. There she was assaulted by a horrible stench and backed out the way she had come in. She thought she had seen Polly on her knees.

Edmund Torres, a new associate, was on his way to Paul Westmoreland's office when he saw Mrs. Holiday walking backwards. "Mrs. Holiday, are you alright?"

"There's something out front," said Mrs. Holiday, and then, without benefit of trash can, went down on one knee and threw up on the rug.

Out front, the man leaned in Polly's direction. "I'll just wait out here." He smiled. "I'll read some of your fine magazines."

Torres moved to Mrs. Holiday's side. "Jesus, Mrs. Holiday," said Torres. He tried to help her up by the elbow but she blurched again. All over his new Allen Edmonds two-hundred-forty-five-dollar Bostonians. Each shoe came in its own soft cotton bag.

What the fuck was going on? Torres opened the door to the reception area and understood everything. Familiar to him from the poverty he had escaped was the odor of unwashed flesh. Old Wine-bag at the bus station.

He tried to breathe only through his mouth as he confronted the man. "Hey, Buddy, you're going to have to move on. You're going to have to move on."

But Buddy wasn't moving on. He looked up and smiled. Waved. "I'm here to see Bob Bateman."

Torres was breathing in little short, shallow breaths. "Bob Bateman. What do you want with Bob Bateman?"

Rutland Atwater was filled with a sunny happiness, a man who had found his vocation. "My name is Rutland Atwater. I'm here to pick up a cashier's check." Except for the smell that accompanied it, his smile could have been described as seraphic.

Polly had crawled out of the reception area only to encounter Mrs. Holiday and her mess. She puked again. Edmund Torres rushed by in the direction of the partners' offices. Doors were slamming, voices were raised.

Steven Perlman, senior partner, strode out of his office, furious. "I'm on the phone with fucking New York in here. What the fuck is going on?"

Polly got unsteadily to her feet, the world was still spinning. She heard voices.

We've got a problem.

What kind of problem?

A stinker in the reception area.

A stinker? Is that a job?

It may be.

Why is he here?

To see Mr. Bateman.

All heads turned to Bob Bateman, who looked as if he might burst. Bob spread his hands. "Don't look at me. I don't know who he is."

Torres knew. "His name is Rutland Atwater. He wants a cashier's check."

Bateman looked at the surrounding faces. "Don't look at me. Call fucking security."

Security's been called.

Call them again.

I saw clients in the hall.

What clients?

Clients who didn't want to come in.

Jesus Christ.

Security's here.

Finally.

But they can't get rid of him.

Why the fuck not?

He handcuffed himself to that little railing.

Undo the fucking handcuffs.

They can't.

Why not?

He swallowed the key.

Fuck me.

We've called building maintenance.

Why?

To dismantle the railing.

Oh, for Christ's sake.

Steve Perlman called Bateman into his office. Westmoreland sidled in as the door shut.

"What the fuck, Bob? What did you bring to work, here?"

"I'm getting blackmailed, Mr. Perlman. I'm not going to take it."

Paul Westmoreland scratched his head. "Uhh, maybe we should, uh . . ."

"Maybe we should what, Paul? Give in to blackmail? Give in to terrorists?"

Westmoreland coughed. "He's hardly a terrorist, Bob—"

"Hold on, gentlemen," said Perlman. "He's here to collect a debt? What debt?"

"An unjustified personal matter."

"How much?"

Bateman stood up straight. "Excuse me, Mr. Perlman. This is a personal matter. Nothing to do with business."

"But you've made it my business, Bob."

There was a knock on the door. Torres stuck his head in. "Yes," said Perlman.

"Excuse me, gentlemen." Torres realized he'd have to play this one carefully. If he ever wanted to make partner. "Uh, uh, Channel Nine is in the building. Ted Sargent. Supposedly, he's on the way up."

Bateman felt a peculiar gurgling. Beneath his Bergdorf Goodman two-hundred-dollar calf-leather belt. His annual bonus liquefying in his duodenum.

Kathryn, Bob's secretary, looked around Torres, knocked at the door. "You've got a call, Mr. Bateman."

"Who?" *Goddamnit.*

"Dick Henry."

Kathryn, betraying nothing of her joy, was having one of the great days. There was that crawling kingsnake vein on Asshole's forehead. Bateman, the rudest, vilest man ever to draw breath, had been through twenty secretaries in three years. But he was a rain-maker and attorneys were never fired anyway. Now he was getting a small fraction of his own. *Enjoy,* Bob.

"Who's Dick Henry?" asked Westmoreland.

Bateman tried to swallow his rage. "I'll take it in my office."

Bateman, hands shaking, picked up his phone. "What the fuck do you want?" he snarled.

Dick, at his own kitchen table, sipped his coffee with apprecia-tion. Splenda *was* as sweet as sugar. Just like they claimed.

"I think you know *what the fuck,* Mr. Bateman. Has Mr. Atwater arrived?"

Bateman cursed a long, vivid blue streak, confirming Dick's opinion that Rutland Atwater, though a singular human being, was indeed a man of value. Right here on his very first matter.

"My advice is this, Mr. Bateman. Go downstairs, to the lobby, and get a cashier's check from City National Bank. Hand it to Mr. Atwater. Isn't it the simplest way?"

CHAPTER THIRTY-TWO

The Diseased, the Demented, and the Damned

The evening moved like molasses toward midnight. Harry Glidden's appetite had gone south, he felt himself growing peevish and petty. Downtown, at work, his famous grasp of case law had seemingly lapsed, leaving him vacant and distracted. Were people looking at him funny? Because once you entertained the thought that people were looking at you funny, you became mannered, clumsy, and insincere. Trying to regain your natural footing, you unconsciously tried to become the person your critics expected you to be—and, whoever that person was, it wasn't you.

Who was Harry Glidden?

He recalled a dream he'd had years earlier. In the dream he'd awoken from a night's slumber, only to remember, with reverberating shock, that he was a murderer. He was a *murderer*!

Sagging with a great fatigue, he stared at the hollow-eyed man in the mirror, an exile from the people of goodness and honesty.

There was no way back.

He would live the years ahead of him in pained acceptance of his new identity: Harry Glidden, one of the diseased, the demented, and the damned.

Then he woke up. The dismal feeling lingered and then he slowly realized, no, *it was all a dream,* oh, good God, it was all a dream! A golden relief coursed through his veins. He rushed to the window, opened it up, gratefully inhaled the crisp morning air. He could still be counted as one of the good people! Harry Glidden, jurist, author, father, husband, good guy. Harry Glidden played for the right team!

But not now.

Now he was an accomplice in a real crime. He looked across the table at Ellen. Eating watermelon. That she salted. She *salted* her watermelon. Who was this woman? Unaffected, unencumbered, capable of sleeping peacefully through the night. He wished he could eat, but he couldn't.

Ellen looked over at her husband. He was giving off that weak-sister vibration. Too late for that shit. "What's wrong with you, Harry?"

He shrugged, enervated and old. *Old.* "Jesus, Ellen. All I can think of is Art Lewis moldering in his walk-in freezer."

"You don't molder in the freezer. That's why he's *in* the freezer." She'd heard of moldering. "What is moldering, Harry?"

"It means to grow mold. I think."

"Like cheese."

"Like cheese." Like stinking raclette. Morning milk separated from afternoon milk by a layer of vegetable ash. Or was that Morbier? In his mind a confused, slimy, green Art Lewis sat up amidst the frozen steaks and chops. "I keep imagining somebody finding out."

"That's why Bernardo is there."

"Suppose Bernardo gets curious?"

"Bernardo is a gardener. He doesn't have a curious bone in his body."

CHAPTER THIRTY-THREE

La Casa de Fantasma

Like I told Ellen Havertine, I wasn't going to let her plan succeed. Too much blood, too many tears. That's why I had again adopted the persona of Dave Hunter, Gas Company employee, and that was why the Gas Company van was rolling through the night. Beside me sat Gas Technician Rojas. Our destination: Temescal Canyon.

I had tried to explain a few details but he wasn't catching on.

"Wait a second, dude. Who's Dick-Dave again?"

I knew I shouldn't have gone there. "Fuck Dick-Dave. All that's important is what we're going to do."

"But who *is* Dick-Dave?"

"Fuck Dick-Dave."

"Sounds like a cracker."

Jesus Christ. I made a turn and there was Art Lewis's place.

"You think the body's in a walk-in freezer?" asked Rojas.

"Only place it can be. That's where they're going to find it when the next part of the scam comes down."

"When he dies again."

"Yup."

"Only a few people ever died twice."

"A few? I only know one. Who else?"

"Well, Lazarus, for one," said Professor Rojas.

"Of course, Lazarus. Who else?"

"The dude in the Beatles. With the bare feet."

"Paul? He didn't die."

"The walrus was Paul."

"So what? He didn't die."

"Oh, yes he did. That's was why he was wearing bare feet to cross the road."

"You mean Abbey Road."

"I mean he was dead."

"He didn't cross the road for the usual reason?"

"What's that?"

"To get to the other side." *Zingo,* Ringo! Got him!

"Fuck you, white man."

"Owned," I chortled, enjoying my victory. According to my son, *owned* was the current word denoting superior cutting skills. Like *burned* had been in my schoolyard days. You just got *burned,* man.

I parked on the street, turned off the engine. We grabbed our tool boxes, walked up to the security gate. I hoped the numbers Pussy had given me were still the right ones.

They were. The gate yawned to full open position, then, as the timer decreed, shut again, quietly, expensively.

Up on the big front porch we waited. There were a few lights on in the house, but no obvious signs of life. But it was a big house so we waited. Chances were the conspirators would leave someone on guard. But maybe not. I took Pussy's key and opened up.

In the kitchen, Bernardo Tavares looked at the walk-in freezers and thought about his orders.

Like many varieties of trouble, the matter had begun with easy money. The couple had called him into the kitchen, bade him sit.

"Bernardo," said Movie Star Lady, "how would you like to earn some extra money?"

"Some *dinero adicional,*" added TV Judge, crucifying the Español.

"Yes, ma'am, yes, sir," he had said. Bernardo was a very good, conscientious gardener, only overcharged the Gliddens by the customary 25 percent. So, obviously, he could use a little more. These were Malibu Beach white people after all. They were filled with guilt. And he was not.

"How much money?" he had inquired respectfully.

TV Judge had exchanged a glance with Movie Star Lady. TV Judge was nervous. Something was up.

"We have a friend who's going out of town for a week or so. We need someone to house-sit. If not all day, at least overnights. It's not far from here, up Temescal Canyon. What do you think?"

Bernardo considered. Tavares Gardening Service, basically himself and *pendejo cabrón* Osvado Rodriguez, had commitments five or six days a week. But overnights, why not?

But why him? How did Movie Star Lady choose him?

Because they didn't know who else to call. There were legitimate, bonded companies that did this. He had friends who did such work. At a quasi-legal minimum, it required lots of paper from the document men down at MacArthur Park.

So why him? Because they needed him. His price clicked upward two notches. They needed him because he was a stupid, opinionless gardener, used to taking orders, grateful for crumbs. "I work seven days, missus," said Bernardo, establishing his fundamental bargaining step.

Movie Star Lady looked at TV Judge, nodded. TV Judge shrugged, uneasy.

Something was indeed up. "I also work nights," lied Bernardo, dolefully, enlarging his fee, "but if you need I make arrangements." Now, how much should he charge? After all, they needed him. He wanted a hundred dollars a night. "Two hundred dollars? Two hundred dollars?"

"Two hundred a night?" Movie Star Lady seemed a little taken aback.

"I have friends maybe help you for one hundred," said Bernardo, with sadness. "But they are *borrachos.*"

Harry looked at his wife. He had reached the ragged perimeter of his Spanish with *dinero adicional.* "What are *borrachos*? Outlaws?"

"No. Drunks."

Goddamnit. He should have learned Spanish like he always promised himself he would. He studied Ellen, shrugged. "Well, we don't need any drunks."

"Okay," said Ellen, nodding at Bernardo. "Two hundred a night."

Bernardo, expressionless, restrained his glee. He'd have done it for seventy-five. For *fifty.* Fifty was good money for sleeping on the couch, watching TV, eating the fine foods in the refrigerator, lifting a cheek and farting aloud when sufficient pressure had accumulated.

"I just watch house, *solamente?*"

"What is *solamente?*" Harry could read Spanish. He knew generally what they were talking about. But not exactly what they were saying.

"Only."

Harry looked at his wife. "How do we, uh . . ." He took Ellen by the wrist. "Excuse us, Bernardo, I need a word with my wife."

Ellen shook off his hand, followed him to the den. "Jesus, Harry. Now he knows something's up."

Harry put a finger over his lips. "Since you're thinking like a Girl Scout, let me think for you. What I want to know is how—"

"—how we make sure he stays out of the walk-in freezer."

"That's right."

"Don't knock the Girl Scouts, Harry."

"Fine. Look. If we warn him to stay out of the freezer, that's exactly where's he going to go first."

"Of course."

"So what *do* we tell him?"

"We tell him there are cameras all over the place and not to go into the freezer."

"Then he goes directly to the freezer."

Ellen thought, then it came to her. "We scare him. The illegals are all superstitious peasants. We scare the shit out of him."

"How are you going to do that?"

TV Judge and Movie Star Lady came back into the kitchen. Now they would lie to him. Okay. He was going to get two hundred dollars a night.

"Bernardo," began Movie Star Lady, "there's a special reason we're going to pay you two hundred dollars a night. *Comprende?*"

Comprendo, white woman.

"We know you are a strong man. *Un hombre fuerte.*"

What kind of silly bullshit was this? Bernardo nodded solemnly. He had spoken English all his life. Good English. In Oaxaca, he had earned a degree in architecture. But up here gardening paid better. Because, for political reasons, his certificate didn't transfer.

"That's why we chose you. There's a ghost in the house. *Uno fanstasmo.*"

You mean, *una fantasma.* But he was supposed to be scared, obviously. He widened his eyes, fashioned his mouth into an O. *"Fantasma,"* he whispered.

Just a superstitious peasant, thought Glidden. He may as well have a bone through his nose.

Ellen continued. "There is an evil ghost in the house. Don't open any doors you don't need to. *No abra el puerto. Necessito.*"

You mean *no abra las puertas.* He widened his eyes a little larger.

"Don't open any doors, cabinets, closets. Eat what's in the refrigerator, and keep your eyes open. I'll leave you my phone number. *Comprende?*"

Oh, I understand, you idiot. There's something in the house. Something I'm not supposed to see. Something my presence will prevent others from seeing. *"Sí. Comprendo."* Now would be a good time to make the sign of the cross, so he did. Then he sighted another opportunity. "Maybe job not for me, missus. I do not want to die."

"You won't die, Bernardo," said TV Judge. "Don't worry."

Bernardo shook his head, rose to his feet, and moaned. "No job, missus. I do not want to die."

"Bernardo, please," said Movie Star Lady.

Bernardo, shaking with fear, made the sign of the cross again and backed out of the kitchen, mumbling.

"Bernardo," said TV Judge, "we'll pay you two-fifty." Shit. They'd talked him into it and right out the other side. He'd have to offer the monkey-eating, fruit-picking savage more money.

Bernardo stopped in his tracks. And settled for two seventy-five.

Now Bernardo studied the walk-in freezers. He had already examined the house from top to bottom. Of course there were no *fantasmas.* Then, standing in just the right place in the kitchen, he had discovered broad scuff marks on the floor, leading from the kitchen door all the way to the left-hand walk-in freezer. Something had been dragged in. Something heavy.

What would you drag to a walk-in freezer? For the first time he felt a chill. *Fantasma.* This was the door. The door he had been encouraged not to open. He grasped the stainless-steel hasp and pulled, the rollers rolled, he felt the rush of frigid air.

He immediately saw what he had not been meant to see. There was a large figure laying on the floor under a frosty, light blue blanket. The man was dead. Had to be. Bernardo approached with caution in any case. He pulled back the blanket.

"Hello, white man." The man was old and had died unshaven and disheveled. There were no obvious signs of foul play. Maybe he'd been sick. But why had no one called the police? The man had been in here a while. Bernardo tugged an arm. Stiff as a statue. *Tieso.* Frozen solid. *Deep-chilled.*

Deep-chilled was what frozen turkeys were called when sold for fresh at Thanksgiving to gullible Americans. Could no one do the math? How do you provide a hundred million fresh turkeys for a single holiday? You froze them. *Tieso.*

Then Bernardo heard the clatter of falling keys. From the entryway. Panic rose into his throat. He yanked the blanket over the dead face and ran out of the freezer.

Two men were waiting for him. He found he had lost the ability to breathe. *"Soy jardinero,"* he croaked. Then something hit him and everything went dark.

Twenty dollars' worth of quarters in a knotted gym sock. Worked every time. It conformed to the shape of the head, conferred maximum concussive power. Like a dead-blow hammer. "What did he say?" I asked.

Rojas looked down on the unconscious man. "He said he was a gardener."

Art Lewis was stiff as a board, unshaven. Blue drugstore slippers. If this man *was* Art Lewis. Of course he was. My plan would work.

I searched through the kitchen drawers. For the right job it's best to have the right tool. But, typically, in the modern home, there is no meat saw.

Ahhh. But here was a Ginsu knife.

I rolled down PCH with Rojas. Mission accomplished. He sparked his chronic, squinted at me.

"So *you're* Dick-Dave."

"I guess so."

He shook his head, looked out the window, turned back. "You know, I never done what you just done."

I looked down at the small tupperware box on the seat between us. "I never done'd it before, either."

"It don't bother you? You know, that day, when the dead come to life and shit, he's gonna be pissed."

"Mr. Lewis or Jesus?"

"Maybe both of them."

CHAPTER THIRTY-FOUR

Infarction

The call had come in at 7:49 in the morning, shattering his dream and chilling his blood. He had been dreaming of Art Lewis. Alive, hale, and hearty. Reports of my death? Exaggerated, laughed the big man. Glidden had been filled with measureless relief. He was still Harry Glidden! The good guy!

Then the phone rang, he sat up, there was Ellen, snoring and oblivious. Thank God Art was still—but, no, he wasn't. The enormous weight was back. He felt a pain in his chest. He picked up the phone, fumbled it. Dial tone.

It rang again as he was making coffee. It was Bernardo. He was quitting. No explanation.

An hour later he served Ellen breakfast. He was trying to be cheery. But he was no actor. He was a clueless stooge who'd been lucky enough to play himself on TV. For twenty-six grand a week. Until it all disappeared.

Ellen looked at him like she had a toothache. "What's wrong now?" she had asked.

"You had a call."

"Who?"

"Bernardo. Bernardo the incurious. He quit."

"What did he say?"

"He just said he was quitting."

"That's all?"

"Almost all."

"What the fuck did he say, Harry?"

"He said *fantasmas*."

Ellen shot out of her seat, threw her plate across the room. "And you just let me sleep?"

"He's a superstitious peasant. Who else sees ghosts?"

"He's been in that fucking freezer." She grabbed her car keys, ran out. Thirty seconds later he heard the screech of tires and she was gone.

He sat there in the silence. For the first time in his life he seriously considered suicide. He had the means. Right upstairs in the closet.

He would open the gun safe, pick up the gun, heavy and cold. He would chamber a shell. Then he would raise the barrel to his temple. Wait a second. He had children. What example would that set? Even if they were adults. Did suicide confer absolution like it used to? In the days of honor and honorable gentlemen?

What was death? Would he be stepping into nothingness? Or stepping through a shroud into the afterlife he had always been promised? Where a loving God would greet him. Where a vindictive God would greet him, fire in his eye, questioning him about Art Lewis. Christ, there was no clean exit for him. If there was an afterlife, he would have to make ready. He would have to confess, perform heartfelt absolution.

That's why Ellen was unmoved. She didn't believe in anything. She was hollow.

The phone rang and he leapt out of his skin. "H-hello?"

"It's me, Harry." It was Ellen. "Everything's under control. Everything's alright."

A wave of blessed relief washed over him. "What happened?"

"Nothing happened," said Ellen. "Art's still in the freezer. Undis-turbed, as far as I can see."

"You're sure?"

"Positive."

"And no one was in the house?"

"No. There're some plates in the kitchen sink. That's all I can see."

"Just Bernardo, in other words."

"That's what I think. Don't worry, Harry. The only thing that went sour is Art dying on us early. And we've dealt with that as best we can. And we're not doing a bad thing. How long did Art have anyway? We didn't give him that heart attack. That's been on the way for years and years."

"I guess so."

"I know so. And tonight, you know what happens tonight?"

"What happens?"

"An infarction. It's time for an infarction."

Ellen, Bobby, and Eileen, back from the desert, looked down on the body of Art Lewis. They'd tried to push it out of the freezer but it wouldn't move.

"Imagine that," said Bobby to Eileen, "your dear husband is stuck to the floor."

"Shut up, Bobby." Eileen loathed him.

Bobby got down on one knee. The body was stuck at the heels, the head, the hands. "What we need is hot water and a spatula, maybe one of those thin pizza-spade things." He looked into the kitchen. "This place'll have everything."

It did have everything. Just like he thought. The hot water did most of the work. Then they dragged the body to the middle of the kitchen floor.

"We've got to lay him out exactly as you found him." Ellen looked at her sister. "Exactly."

"Why does it fucking matter?" Eileen flared, nervous. Fucking Ellen had to control everything.

"So any trauma experienced in the fall will be reflected in the way they'll find him." Ellen looked at her imbecile sister. Anybody could be a nurse. All you needed was a pulse.

"Well, you saw. He was flat on his back. Arms out."

"Alright. Let's get a story together." Ellen considered the corpse. "Uh, he comes down from upstairs, he goes to the refrigerator, he gets dizzy, he falls backwards. That's where Eileen finds him."

Eileen had a better idea. "Why don't we roll him down the stairs? So he lands naturally?"

"Because I don't want to carry him *up the stairs,* you moron. Do you?"

"No."

"Then shut up and let me do the thinking."

"Yeah," added Bobby.

"Shut up, Bobby." Eileen hated everyone.

Bobby grinned. "And he wouldn't roll naturally, Eileen, you cluck. He's frozen like a bowling pin."

"SHUT UP, Bobby."

"Both of you shut up." Ellen would kill them both. Slowly. What was fate telling her when, in the moment of supreme crisis, she found two halfwits by her side?

Then Bobby noticed an odd thing. In the pushing and shoving, one of Lewis's blue, heelless slippers had come off. Bobby pointed to Lewis's left foot. "What the fuck is that?"

Ellen didn't see. "What are you talking about?"

Bobby stared. Yes. He was looking at concentric rings of pink and white. "Fucker's missing a toe."

Unquestionably, to all, it was gone.

"When did that happen?" asked Eileen.

Bobby shook his head. "After he was dead, you clam. You don't have exposed bone on your body."

Ellen stared, thinking. "Bernardo quit this morning."

Bobby nodded. "There's your man."

"*Who's* your man?" Eileen whined, fists clenched.

Finally everything was arranged as well as it could be. Art's limbs, still frozen, resisted natural placement. That would take time. They stuffed Art's pajamas with paper towels, which looked odd and puffy. But the purpose was to absorb any moisture defrosting would produce. It would be strange for a corpse to be found in wet pajamas. In his own kitchen.

Bobby looked down on the rich, legally alive, dead man. "How long will it take him to thaw out?"

"A couple of days," said Eileen, back on familiar medical ground. "At room temperature."

Bobby nodded. "Sure. Like any other two hundred and thirty-five pound Thanksgiving turkey."

This was Eileen's last straw. "Ellen, would you make him shut up, please? *Please?*"

Ellen stamped her foot. "Both of you assholes shut up."

"Sorry," said Bobby, "I didn't mean Thanksgiving turkey."

"Apology accepted," said Eileen, in the spirit of peace.

"I meant Christmas turkey." Bobby grinned, triumphant.

"BOTH OF YOU ASSHOLES SHUT UP."

Bobby shrugged extravagently. "Sorry. I didn't mean to speak ill of Eileen's poor, mutilated husband. But what about the medical examiner? How does he not notice the toe that isn't there?"

"He doesn't notice because we appoint our own medical examiner." Yes, thought Ellen. The good man had already been chosen.

"You can do that?"

Ellen nodded. "Harry can."

Eileen's head was spinning. "Will someone *please* tell me what's going on? *Who* can do *what?*"

"Shut up, Eileen." Bobby and Ellen spoke at the same time.

CHAPTER THIRTY-FIVE

Did You Know Mr. Lewis?

Pussy swept up the hair, rinsed out the big sink, disinfected the waist-high, stainless-steel stand-alone platform where Dr. Peach's patients were clipped, cleaned, and groomed. Then she walked up Abbot Kinney to get a taco.

In the furthest reaches of her imagination she had never entertained pet care as an occupation. In fact, she had laughed with Violet and Wendy and the other girls at the Zebra Club about the world's most pitiful profession: mobile dog grooming. *Yuck.*

I just see one of those trucks and I sneeze.

The tacos carnitas at Abbot's were pretty good and the onion rings, if you ate them quickly and sparingly, were good, too.

Working for Dr. Peach was one of the most normal jobs she'd ever had. And the funny part of it was the animals, they *wanted* to be clean. You could see that they felt better. Carried their newly fluffed-out tails higher. Not like they walked in, head down, embarrassed, all matted and dumpy. Their eyes got all sparky, you could see, when she was finished. They wanted to thank her. And she would rub that little groove high on their noses, between their eyes. And they would roll their shoulders around, try to smile.

She paid the Mexican girl, started back down the street. Some big, dirty slob was selling incense in front of that expensive dress place.

The slob looked her up and down, then smiled with some screwed-up teeth. "How 'bout some Pondicherry Pine, lassie?" He had some bullshit Jamaican accent. "Or some Montego Sweet Cedar?"

You gotta be kidding, dude. She had long ago learned to judge a man's character quickly. In three seconds flat. She stopped, raised her sunglasses, delivered her summation. "Fuck off, loser."

She walked back to Cat & Dog.

"Were those fish tacos great or what?" inquired Dr. Peach.

"Fantastic," said Puss, slipping into her smock.

And so the afternoon had begun, one hour gliding into the next, to the hum of newsradio. She looked into the deep, wise brown eyes of Jaboc, a very large German shepherd, and played with his ears while Dr. Peach fiddled and probed in the rear. It was amazing what an animal would accept at his hands.

"You've got quite a way with animals, Miss Grafton."

"Thank you, Doctor."

Dr. Peach peeled off his gloves. "Don't call me doctor anymore. My name is Clark."

"Thank you, Doctor." She giggled. "I mean *Clark*."

"And what do I call you, Miss Grafton? Besides Miss Grafton. Which I'll happily continue if you wish."

"Uh . . ." Color had come to her face. ". . . call me Pu—uh, Penelope."

Clark smiled. "I've always loved that name."

"Thank you, Doctor." There was a pause. "I mean *Clark*." They both had laughed again.

Then she became aware of the radio.

"This just in to KFWB. Developer Art Lewis, married just five days go, has apparently died of a heart attack."

Suddenly her eyes were full and she couldn't see.

Dr. Peach watched her. "I'm sorry, Penelope. Did you know Mr. Lewis?"

CHAPTER THIRTY-SIX

Bella da Costa Greene

I'd met Nedra at a club on Pico, east of La Cienega. It was called the Mint. It had a nice bar running down the starboard side, with the requisite mirrors for observing your fellow drinkers. Angle of incidence equals angle of reflection.

But I wasn't there to drink. I was there to see Delta Freight. They were friends of mine, currently a blues band.

Naturally, I distrusted white blues. The blues was a mysterious entity. The structure was deceptively simple, accessible enough for many thousands of musicians to conclude that yes, they could do that, too.

But the artistry inherent in the work of Muddy Waters, Howlin' Wolf, Hubert Sumlin, Little Walter, Freddie King, B.B. King, Albert King, Jimmy Reed, Jimi Hendrix, that artistry was exceedingly difficult to quantify. And more difficult to reproduce. Suffice to say they knew what to leave in, and, more important, what to leave out.

I had been among the multitude who had concluded *I could do that, too.* The I-IV-V. Then I heard a Jimmy Reed tune.

> *I walk the streets at night, baby*
> *I got nothin' else to do*

With sudden shame I recalled the unfortunates I had pitied in my travels, watching them trudge slowly over downtown streets at two in the morning. Where the fuck were they going?

They were walking, that's what.

So, white blues. White blues, with rare exceptions, Clapton, Stevie Ray Vaughan, Johnny Winter, and a few others, maybe Kenny Wayne Shepherd, came hand in hand with cultural imperialism. The natives had stumbled on something interesting, let us improve and exploit it. Let us expand it, refine it, remodel it, substitute cleverer chords, and play it better. And longer. Much longer.

The result was blooze. A windy cacophony that started in the middle and ended in the middle. When someone begged them to stop. A little went a very long way.

Meanwhile, the original purveyors looked on in stoic silence. Thus, I had no substantial hopes for Delta Freight.

But while they were setting up, a tall, black girl took the stage with a piano player. She was introduced as Nedra. She reached for the microphone and pulled it close.

Nedra's voice was not large but it cut me to the quick. Slightly sandy, yet precise and inventive, she stated simple truths simply, in a manner that drew me right in.

Is that all there is?

She sang one song then reclaimed her seat at the bar. Our eyes met in the mirror. Impelled by a force that overwhelmed my natural wretchedness in the presence of beauty, I went over and sat beside her.

She was dressed plainly, no rings on her fingers. "Yes?" she said.

"I'm Dick Henry," I said. "And that was one of the most beautiful things I've ever heard." I looked into her brown eyes. "I don't know what to say next, because I'm not very smart, but I wanted to tell you that while I still could."

She looked at me solemnly and then a delighted peal of melodious laughter burst forth and suddenly we were very present to one another.

Delta Freight took that exact moment to mount the attack. *"What the fuck, LOS ANGELES,"* bellowed the tattooed, bandannaed lead singer at the top of his lungs, adjusting his basket. "We're gonna do a blues forya."

I had three seconds to talk to Nedra or have our unique moment blown away forever. I grabbed her hand. "Let's go get some Chinese food."

Nedra looked over at Delta Freight. "Okay."

On the downbeat we hustled through the black curtain into the cool and quiet of nighttime Pico Boulevard.

"They'll never know we're gone," I said, acknowledging our conspiracy.

Nedra laughed again.

"So, where do you want to go, Dick?"

"Ah Fong's."

Where we danced.

Nedra and I didn't ask a lot of questions, we just drifted in a golden haze. She loved words and so did I, and we reveled in our exchange. Even though she knew many more of them. I was twenty-seven years old, recently discharged from the nuclear Navy, honorably. She was twenty-four, had graduated from an Ivy League college on scholarship. I always felt on tiptoes in her company; she was smarter, better educated.

The fact that she came to care about me amazed and astounded me. I couldn't believe my luck. It had to be karma, because I'd done nothing in this present life to deserve her. I felt exalted, felt that the future had indeed been loosed. I could end up someplace incomprehensible to the ordinary creature I had been just weeks ago.

Physically, we partook of an incendiary mutual desire. I wanted to be in her, through her, of her. I couldn't get enough. *We* couldn't get enough. Together we went out into the world possessed of the most delicious of secrets—that we had ascended to Olympian heights, that we traveled and traversed where others could not. Where others could not imagine.

Sweetest of all things was her nickname for me. She demanded my whole name: Richard Hudson Henry, then thought about it. I'm going to call you Hud, she said.

Like Paul Newman. I loved it. And I loved her. And I informed her of the fact, fervently, ten times a day.

Did she love me? Yes. How do I know? Because she told me only once. Just once. Once. *I love you, Hud.*

From today's vantage point, I see that various, unquestioned assumptions of mine had imperceptibly hardened into certitude. That fact that our relationship had been constructed from the outside in, exoskeletonary, rather than from the inside out, made it fragile, made it susceptible to shock. And when that shock happened, in due course, there was no structure inside to bear the weight. But I knew none of that.

Johnnie Cochran has gone on to say that everything in America is about race. I wouldn't have believed it back then and now I don't want to believe it. But it isn't for me to say. All I knew was that I had never, to my knowledge, allowed race to be a point of distinction in my personal affairs. Men were men. It was the content of character that was important.

Nedra's affection had raised myself in my own view. Perhaps I was capable of higher things. Shortcuthood, as a vocation, lay undefined before me, not yet a real choice. Maybe I would go back to school. Learn to write. Explore geology. Or anthropology.

Nedra was a writer. Determined to break Hollywood wide open. I had no doubt she would. One day I brought her a fascinating story I'd come across.

Bella da Costa Greene had been hired in 1905 to be J. P. Morgan's personal librarian. Her job expanded greatly with her demonstrated capability. She worked the rest of her life for Morgan and his family and was rumored to have been the great man's mistress. What made the story unique was Miss da Costa's race. She was black. But because of her beauty and education and light complexion, she had conducted her professional life as a white woman.

I brought this story to Nedra. "If you leave out the black-tragedy aspect of this, I think it would make a great movie."

Nedra hesitated. "The black-tragedy aspect? What's that?"

"What I meant was, if you just stuck to *her* story, a woman normally assumed to be powerless possessing a huge and usable power, that would make a good movie. What she did with that power."

"And the black-tragedy aspect?"

The ground had grown unstable beneath my feet but I didn't know it. "That would be slavery, Jim Crow stuff, stuff that happened, but stuff that would change the pure power of this story. Of course, that all happened. But what I'm saying—"

Nedra had slowly pushed herself up from her seat at the kitchen table. Her face terrified me.

"You *white people,*" she hissed, bitterness dripping from every syllable, directed at *me.* "You *white people.* You *white people* don't know a thing about us. You don't know *a thing about us.* But we have to know *you.* We have to know *everything about you.* What you *really mean* when you say this, what you *really mean* when you say that . . ."

What Nedra said after that I don't remember. I can't remember. But it came on and on, a horrifying, hidden, supperating wound lanced. I stood naked in the torrent. After a while I numbly realized I couldn't listen to any more. I found my way down her wooden stairs and walked out under the California sun. I was scalded, scorched.

Disconnected portions of her words floated through my mind, setting phantom dialogue adrift.

You know us but we don't know you, Nedra? Maybe I do know nothing. I'll give you that. But how can you claim to know me if you don't realize *my ignorance*? That there're things I just don't know? How would I know the depths of the pain you swallow with your daily bread? How would I know? How *could* I know? But how could you, brilliant as you are, flaming torch to my candle, how could you just assume I *did* know? How could you assume I knew and didn't care? How *could* you? How could you, dear?

I'd read Douglass and Du Bois and Malcolm X at her urging. I knew of chattel, I knew of people with no last names, of families ripped viciously asunder, I knew of murder and mayhem, I knew of the artificial hierarchy of house and field, and the terrible price of impudence. *Impudence.* A condition found anywhere an overseer might glance on a bad morning.

I knew a lot of facts, but in the end, though, I didn't know shit.

Nedra and I were ruined.

Blind mutual forgiveness is the only answer. The fault may be mine, in the larger sense, but the problem is *ours.* And that's asking more of others than of me. But what else could be the solution? If there is one. What was done was wrong. How do we go back? A country built on the free labor of unfree men? Yes. That's what happened. But how to settle things now? We need a Solomon. I'm just the Shortcut Man.

True love is as big as the imagination, limitless. I walked out of Nedra's house, my heart in splinters, my imagination smashed. I walked into a smaller world, bereft of hope and wonder.

A biblical seven-day deluge commenced as I reached my car. I drove home shivering. But still on fire.

Cinders. I had believed, soul deep, albeit without examination, that love would trump race when they met in the alley. But no. Race kicked love's ass. What other icebergs had I missed?

Johnnie Cochran passed on to his great reward. I hope, for his sake, for my sake, for our sake, that race means nothing up there. That there is no race. But the afterlife will be populated by the same fools that prate and prattle down here. I'm not optimistic.

That's how Nedra and I were destroyed. And this wouldn't be on my mind except for this morning's call from Robert Patrick.

Patrick assured me that further misunderstandings concerning Ms. Scott's fundamental right to live where she pleased would never see the light of day. However, continued Patrick, Azure Gardens would go up one way or the other. Civic momentum, once engaged, could not be stopped. Bledsoe was doomed, done for.

But, perhaps, since I knew Nedra Scott, he reasoned, I could talk sense to her. Her property might be worth a hundred grand viewed through rose-colored glasses. He had a pair. His top offer might conceivably reach five hundred thousand. A pleasing percentage would be paid me if I could convince her to do the right thing.

Obviously, Mr. Patrick did not know of what he asked, but I said I would give it a try.

Someone said most men do not marry the woman in their lives whom they love the most. Maybe, like magnetism, love is both attractive and repulsive. So it's not that you don't, you *can't*. I had been banished from heaven. But, like a chess piece across the field of time and distance, Georgette came forward one square at a time. The rest was history.

CHAPTER THIRTY-SEVEN

Ed Huff

Two full days had passed. Ellen looked down at Art. He was ready to entertain. He lay pliable, arms spread wide on the kitchen floor.

At the kitchen table, red-eyed and sobbing, Eileen was making her big moment as big as possible. Ellen looked over from the sink. Eileen's tears dredged up the long-held desire to slap the piss out of her. In this case, however, Eileen was performing as ordered. Cry, bitch, cry.

In the library, Harry Glidden resisted the impulse to watch the Lakers. Then the doorbell rang.

Ellen beat him to the front door, opened up. A small, balding man with a receding chin held a black bag. This would be asshole Ed Huff.

The man stuck his hand out. "I'm Ed Huff," he said. "And I'm so sorry."

Ellen stepped forward, pulled Huff's head into her perfumed bosom. "Oh, Dr. Huff, thank you so much for coming." She let loose a few tears, finally let him up for air.

Huff met with Judge Glidden in the library.

"What we want here, Ed, is privacy. You can see Eileen is heartbroken." Well, you could *hear* it. "We don't need a CSI investigation, microscopes up Art's ass. We want dignity. Dignity for a great man, cut down at his moment of supreme happiness."

Huff nodded. "I understand completely. And I agree completely. But, as far as the certificate—"

"I can sign, Ed. As an officer of the court. If that's good enough for you."

"Oh. *Fine.* That would be fine with me."

"Great."

Judge Glidden reached into his jacket pocket, removed his checkbook, opened it. Carefully he detached a check to Dr. Ed Huff, $10,000. He handed it to Huff.

Huff looked at the check. "I can't accept this."

"Why not?"

"It's the grief talking. It's too much." Ed held out the check in return.

But Glidden folded Huff's fingers back around the check. "Take it, Ed. With my thanks and gratitude." The check disappeared into Huff's coat pocket.

Huff began his inspection. In med school he'd done some forensics but that was a while ago. Quite a while. The man was dead. That was certain. And he was cold. Maybe he should check internal temp. But that meant inserting a clean instrument up the dead man's hairy ass. Shit, the man was dead.

He was acutely aware that Ellen Havertine was kneeling down across the body from him. Every time he looked up, it was into Ellen Havertine's bosom. Which would be righteously classified as a *rack.* He could almost see a nipple.

"Is there a problem, Doctor?"

Huff wrenched his eyes northward. "Uhhh, no. I mean, he's a little cold."

Miss Havertine nodded. "You'd think he was *dead.*"

Huff open and shut his mouth like a fish. He'd almost laughed. Was she serious?

"I guess he came down for a sandwich." The actress took a deep breath, straining the fabric.

He watched Miss Havertine's eyes mist over. *Eyes.* If only he had chameleon eyes. So he could look at two things at once. Her chest and her face. Then maybe he would understand what she was saying. Someone had eaten a sandwich. *He* would eat a sandwich. Later. Meat loaf. If it hadn't gone bad.

The judge watched Ellen hypnotize Huff with the community property, 36C. Art's socks were never removed. And the doctor didn't see the sugar ants that crawled out of Art's hair and meandered down his forehead. Ellen had blown them off with a perfect theatrical sneeze. Which meant what, wondered Glidden, hundreds of them? Can't tickle a dead man. Ants. Like soldiers moving through a dense forest. The judge squirmed, ran fingers through his hair.

Finally the procedure was complete, the body on its way to the brothers McKinley. Huff sat at the kitchen counter, signed a document, handed it to Judge Glidden. "Here we go, Harry. All taken care of." He shook the judge's hand. "I'm sincerely sorry about your—your brother-in-law?"

Glidden nodded sorrowfully. Brother-in-law was a paper relationship under the best of terms. And he was once removed. "Thank you, Ed." He looked at the floor. He'd learned aspects of sorrow on *Special Counsel*. Knit your eyebrows and look down, shake your head a bit. He shook his head a bit.

He put a hand on Huff's shoulder. "I knew you'd be here for me, Ed. And for Art Lewis. Thank you from the bottom of my heart. You've been a true friend."

Then Ellen had come up, bosomed him again, sprinkled a few more tears. "Some things are better kept in-house, so to speak," said Huff. "Away from the vultures and hyenas." The good doctor paused. "By the way, Harry. You playing in that tournament at Riviera?"

The Victims of Violent Crime Benefit. "Why, yes. Yes, I am. With Ted Sargent. You have time, Ed?"

"Time for what?" Incredulous Huff.

"A spot in the foursome?"

"*Is* there a spot?"

"For you there is, Ed."

"Whoa. No kidding?"

"No kidding."

"Ted Sargent?"

"Ted Sargent. The one and only."

"I'm in?"

"You're in if you want, Ed-man."

"Well—then I'm in."

Glidden clapped him on the shoulder. "I'll see you there."

Huff had departed. Ellen and Harry came back into the kitchen. Eileen was still sobbing.

Ellen looked at her sister. Enough was enough. "Eileen?"

Eileen stopped, mid-sob. "Y-y-yes?"

"Shut up."

CHAPTER THIRTY-EIGHT

Fame

Bobby do this. Bobby do that. Bobby clean up this. Bobby clean up that. It was all bullshit. Ellen's perpetual incompetence. But for a million-dollar share—he'd put up with her.

He parked the Infiniti on Yucca, within sight of Ivar. He checked for the gun in his coat pocket. There it was. And it *was* loaded, he didn't have go through that. He'd gone through it ten times back at the apartment.

Showtime.

But a hit first. Two hits. Okay, three. This was a serious mission. He slipped on the brown DHL jacket.

If Ivar wasn't the steepest street in Los Angeles, it was in the top ten. And somewhere up there, on the left-hand side of the street, was 1863.

He'd knock. A man would open up. Are you Bernardo? he would ask. I have a package for him. As he handed the package to the man he'd pull out the gun and shoot Bernardo in the head. With a second bullet for the professional Luca Brasi finality of it all.

Or maybe he'd knock, ask the man if he were Bernardo, then ask another question. You cut off Art Lewis's toe? Bernardo's guilty mouth would fall open and he'd shoot him right between the eyes. Then he'd walk back down the hill. Two minutes later he'd be back in his apartment, where a big rock waited for him on top of that Coltrane CD. *A Love Supreme*. Yes, indeed. A man and his pipe. That was love, baby.

It *had* to be the steepest street in Los Angeles. Fuck Fargo Street. Finally he reached 1863. He paused to breathe. It hurt. His lungs were probably brittle with cocaine. What he needed was more cocaine. Showtime.

He had to admit, it was a ballsy move for a gardener. Maybe he'd used pruning shears. One little snip, then a call for a hundred thousand dollars. Except there'd been no call. The dude was playing it close to the chest. But why had he quit so suddenly? Why else. Because he was the Snipper.

Snipper, meet Sniper.

He knocked and after a bit the door drew back. If this were Bernardo he was a nice-looking man. An honest, square face, hazel eyes, a full head of curly black hair, and a ready smile with repairs in gold.

"Are you Bernardo Tavares?"

Before the man answered, a little girl, maybe four, came up and hid behind his leg, looking around at Bobby, smiling, then hiding again.

"Can I help you?" asked the man.

"You're Bernardo?"

The man patted the little girl's head. "Maybe I am Bernardo. Who are you?"

Suddenly the man recognized Bobby. Recognized him with delight. "You are Bobby Lebow! *You are Bobby Lebow!*" He turned to yell into the interior. "*Lourdes, apúrate y salga!* It's Bobby Lebow!"

There was a shriek and a stampede of feet. Four children arrived with a good-looking woman bringing up the rear. The children would not have been more excited at the circus. The woman shrieked again. "Bobby Lebow! Bobby Lebow!"

Bernardo clapped him on the shoulder. "*Me, Dad, and Me* was my favorite show. But you the best. The *best.*" He turned to his wife. "Didn't I always say that Bobby Lebow the best? Didn't I?"

"Yes, you did! Yes, you always did! The very best. And I agreeeeee!"

The kids squirted out past Bobby to disseminate the news. The apartment next door was opened by another child. "Bobby Lebow is here!" screamed Bernardo Junior.

"Who is that?" returned the girl at the door.

"I don't know," said Bernardo Junior, "but he's here!"

Two minutes later, Bobby and twenty-five residents of 1863 were crammed into Bernardo's. Bernardo directed his wife to break out the special bottle of tequila he had been saving. Lourdes did as ordered and more tequila came from next door. All the men salted their thumbs, bit into their lemons, and drank tequila with Bobby Lebow. Bobby was only going to have one, but before he knew it he'd swallowed four. Someone thrust a guitar into his hands and he sang. And sang again. Digital cameras took pictures, printers printed them, Bobby signed them. Eventually, Bobby remembered what was waiting on top of *A Love Supreme* and extricated himself with handshakes, hugs, and promises to return.

Momentum carried him down the street. At the corner he ran. The Infiniti started right up.

Back at Bernardo's the excitement slowly cooled from white-hot to red-hot to, now, a gentle, dull, satisfied crimson.

Bernardo scratched his head.

"What?" asked Lourdes, his wife.

"I forgot to ask something important to Mr. Bobby Lebow."

"Ask him what?"

Bernardo finished off the dregs of the tequila. "I forgot to ask him why he come here." Fuck Movie Star Lady and TV Judge. Who had their noses high in the air. Hiding their stiff in the freezer.

Bobby Lebow. Bobby Lebow was good people.

CHAPTER THIRTY-NINE

Side by Side

I dropped by Electric Avenue. Dennis had just about finished up my commission. I looked at the paintings side by side. As always, I couldn't tell the difference. It was beautiful work and I told him so.

Honest praise lightened his load for a minute. "It is good work," he agreed. He looked down at them. "I hope whoever is going to get it deserves it."

You don't know the half of it, my friend.

He told me his plans. He couldn't stay here at Electric Avenue. Where was he going to go? He wasn't sure. Maybe New Mexico.

Sante Fe is a nice place for artists.

Yeah, but it might be stuffy. Maybe Mexico.

Why Mexico? What do you know about Mexico?

Don't know nothin' about Mexico. That's why I'm goin'.

He rolled up a fattie. Did I want a hit? No, thanks. He lit up, breathed deep.

That's how I left him, wrapped in his dreams.

CHAPTER FORTY

Encopresis

The purpose of the toe, of course, was leverage. Physiognomically and in the matter at hand. To stop the circus by bringing attention to the strange death of Art Lewis. Someone, unless the fix were in, would question a body with a sawed-off toe. And that attention would eventually blow the posthumous marriage and the estate grab out of the water.

It was time for a paperwork harvest. The first crop to come in was a tax summary on the Gliddens' Malibu Beach property. They were two years behind. Which meant they were broke. Which suggested a motive for the whole scam.

Then, through my informal downtown network, I received a fax copy of the death cert. I would send my best wishes and a honeybee to Brendy Salinas.

The cert was signed by Dr. Edward Huff. And Harry J. Glidden. Which was enough for the coroner to buy it off. The fix was in.

Which changed the value of the toe. Obviously, it had not called itself to the attention of Dr. Huff. It didn't matter why. By intent or incompetence he was now at the heart of the matter. Forcing me to throw the toe into the gears of progress.

The weak link would be Dr. Huff, who wouldn't know what was really on the line. I googled Huff and up came a picture of Huff and Glidden on a golf course and a piece of video on YouTube from Channel 9. In the photo, Huff basked in the reflected glory of the great Judge Glidden.

I looked up the conscientious Dr. Huff. He was an ear, nose, and throat man working out of Cedars-Sinai.

I called him up, told his assistant it was a dire emergency. A minute later he picked up.

"This is Dr. Huff. How can I help you?"

"This is Dr. Gruff."

"Dr. Gruff?"

"I need to speak to Dr. Huff."

"This *is* Dr. Huff."

"This is Dr. Gruff."

"This is Dr. Huff."

"This is Dr. Gruff."

"Is this some kind of game?"

"Like the game you played with Art Lewis?" I launched into business.

"What are you talking about?"

"I'm looking at a death certificate with your name on it."

"Who are you?"

"You're Edward B. Huff?"

"Who is this?"

"Apparently, Mr. Huff, you didn't notice Mr. Lewis was missing a toe."

"Missing a toe?"

"The little toe. Sawed off at the metacarpal. Bone plainly exposed. How do you explain that?"

"I don't know what you're talking about."

"I believe you, Doctor. Because you didn't look. Or you didn't see. I smell money."

"Who is this?"

"This is someone who's going to fuck up your party big-time. Someone who's going to drag you *right into hell.* Someone who knows, to the very minute, how long Art Lewis had been dead."

A hoarse whisper. "I don't know anything about any of this."

"Well, I do. Do you know what Mr. Lewis said when I cut off his toe?"

"You?" His voice quavered with fear.

"Answer me, Huff. What did Mr. Lewis say when I cut off his toe?"

"W-w-what did he say?"

"He didn't say a word. Because he'd been dead for *three days.*" I let the horror sink in. If you weren't used to dealing with threats, a threat would deeply frighten. "I'll be calling you with instructions, Huff. Goodbye." I hung up.

Huff set the phone in the cradle but did not have the strength to rise. His breath came shallow and weak, his brain didn't work. His anus felt loose and he wondered if he'd soiled himself.

He put his hands on his desk, pulled himself out of his three-thousand-dollar brass-studded leather chair and shouted something at the top of his lungs. There was an unaccustomed warmness in his pants. Something was running down his leg. From med school, a word floated to consciousness. *Encopresis.* Involuntary shitting. Now he knew how it might come about.

Mrs. Ingram entered his office, alarm on her face. "Doctor, are you alright?"

"GET OUT!" he screamed.

Her mouth dropped open and out she went.

He sagged into his seat, felt his feces conform to his posture. Yuck. He rose back up instantly. His mind had started to return. Issues, issues, decisions. He must make decisions.

First, his pants.

In his private bathroom he cleaned up as best he could. The soiled underwear he would throw away. He looked at himself in the mirror. Come on, Ed. *Come on.* Take a deep breath. Straighten the spine. Think. Think.

As for Art Lewis, he hadn't really checked a goddamn thing. Lewis was well beyond the Hippocratic oath. The man was dead, for chrissake. He'd taken Glidden's word for everything, basically. Glidden was a goddamn judge! And his name was on the cert, too. Thank God! Another name. Had the mystery man called Glidden as well?

What had Eileen Lewis said? Her husband must have come down from upstairs, rummaged around in the fridge, then fell back, hitting his head. Which killed him. Was that all bullshit? How could it be bullshit? Were they all lying? Ed Huff, chump of chumps?

He inhaled, exhaled raggedly. He checked his watch. Glidden would be downtown. He'd call his office.

"Judge Glidden's office."

"Yes, is Judge Glidden in?"

"I'm sorry, he's in the courtroom. Could I leave him a message?"

"Yes, please. This is Ed Huff. *Doctor* Ed Huff. And this is a dire emergency. I need to speak to the judge as soon as possible. I can't stress the urgency of this matter. This is of the utmost urgency."

"Is this a medical emergency, Doctor?"

"Uh, no."

"Then I'll give him your message at break, Doctor. What's your number?"

He'd given his number, hung up, and then the fear came back. He ran for the toilet.

CHAPTER FORTY-ONE

The Second Mrs. Glidden

Not two minutes after I'd hung up with Huff there was a knock at my door. I looked through the side window. It was Ellen Glidden. Well, well, well. Monty Hall. Let's make a deal.

I opened up. She smiled at me. A professional smile. I could tell the difference. "Hi, Dick-Dave. Can we talk?"

I stepped back, gestured her in. "The second Mrs. Glidden."

She took a careful seat on the couch, looked around. "You rent, of course?"

"Why would that be your business?"

"Because I want to make sure you own."

"Do you."

"At least your house."

"I don't think there's common ground between us."

"There's always common ground between people of reason."

"Did you bring a big bag of money?"

"Is that what you want?"

She looked into my eyes like she was seeing my soul. Of course, it was technique. But her technique was flawless. That's why she'd accomplished what she had accomplished. In three seconds she promised me love, devotion, and the best ball-cupping, perfumed hand, desperate, hungry blow job I'd ever get in this lifetime. I'd spew my seed across the sky.

She saw me receive her message. She smiled.

The consciousness of a human being is bicameral. The mind is one part, the body, the mind's wordless equal, the second. Communication with another person is always both mind-to-mind *and* body-to-body. Unless this dualism is shocked into its ingredients, we operate in perfect, unknowing synchrony, never suspecting that *we are two.* But the Shortcut Man knew. The Shortcut Man had been torn asunder with fear . . . and with pleasure. Cock of iron, feet of clay.

I looked at her and felt my body twist in the wind of her desire and I thirsted.

She opened a button on her shirt, showed me a little cleavage. "You ever make love to a movie star, Dick?"

Every call Harry got was a fucking emergency. He looked at the yellow slip. There were no normal calls in his celebrity life. But Huff? Why now? Why a dire emergency? A shard of panic creased his mind. He hoped Huff wasn't a cunt. But, of course, that was why he'd been pressed into service. Huff was a perfect cunt.

Arnelle put her head in. "Patricia on line seven."

Arnelle had been around for the great marital changeover. To all outward appearances she was neutral. At the bottom he knew she rooted for Patricia. An anger at the world surged within him and he picked up the phone.

"Hi, Patricia." Clipped. Businesslike.

"Did you talk with Monica?"

"Should I?"

"She needs a new car, Harry. Don't you think you should help her out?"

"Since when did our children become helpless adults?"

"Her car was stolen and they wrecked it. She wasn't prepared for this."

"That's why there's a thing called insurance. For accidents, for thefts, for shit just like this."

A pleased thread crept into her tone. "Did I catch you at a bad time, Harry?"

"What did you really call about?"

"Are you alright, Harry?"

"Goddamnit, I'm fine."

"Are you taking your fish oil?"

"You did not call in the middle of my goddamn busy day to talk about *fish oil*." It was the fear of the unknown, Huff's emergency, that had ignited dark clouds of unease into anger. Point to Patricia. He consciously tried to tamp down his sudden hatred.

"Actually, dear, I called to inquire as to when I might expect my painting. The Kostadi?"

Fuck you, Patricia.

Her reminder was supposed to hurt but it didn't. In fact, the reverse. The naked depth of her anger and hurt almost quenched his own with vicious satisfaction. *Kostadi.* She had mispronounced Kostabi's name with purpose—to show how little she truly cared for the artist or the work she'd managed to wring out of him during the last minutes of their marriage. Possession is nine-tenths of the law, darling. And you'll never have it, you bitch.

"Maybe a week, I'll have it for you. A week or so. I know how you've always loved Kostadi."

After a marriage of that length, you were never truly unmarried. Some rounds had less action than others, but the fight never ended until God threw in the towel. "Why don't you let me just keep the goddamn thing, Patricia? You don't give a shit about it."

"Why don't you truly ask me, Harry?" she rejoined. "With a little humility? With a little humanity?"

He was filled with a grinding frustration. He had pretty much spent his humanity as of late. He was a grabber, a grasper, a grifter, a felon in noble black robes. "Patricia . . ."—his voice quavered for a millisecond—". . . Patricia, please give me my painting."

Silence on the line. "Patricia? Patricia, are you there?"

"You really want it, Harry?" Her voice had grown soft, with that smoker's graininess. From that surgically tightened throat. Wreathed in scarves and shawls.

"Give me the painting."

Another pause.

"No, Harry. You can't have it. And Feldman says you've got a week to deliver or he files."

Then she hung up. He threw the phone, county-provided, across the room. But it didn't break. The piece of shit would fall apart during an important call, but thrown at a fucking wall? In that circumstance it was solid as a stone. Life, baby. What had he heard about life? That was it: *You're born, things go bad for a while, then you die.* Fuck it.

But first things first. He'd call Henry, the Shortcut Man, jerk his chain, check on delivery.

Then that twat, Huff.

There is a certain, definable moment in the accommodation of evil that requires tacit acceptance and approval. Seconds past that instant of decision the river Morpheus flows swiftly to the unconscious.

But I couldn't do it. I could be bought. I'd *been* bought. But not outright, brazenly, on the barrelhead.

"Get the fuck out of here, Mrs. Glidden."

Her sexiness dropped away like a sheet. Cold anger flooded into her beautiful, ugly face.

I was ready for Krakatoa but my phone rang. *H. Glidden.*

What a fine coincidence. I looked over at Ellen. The phone call had injected reality into our private world of desire and contempt. "I'm going to take this outside," I told her.

I stepped out on the porch, answered. "This is Dick."

"This is Judge Glidden."

"What can I do for you, Judge?"

"I think you know."

I ventured out on the ice. "The Kostabi is ready."

"Good."

I heard the evil satisfaction in his voice. Maybe he'd just talked to his ex.

"How did it come out, Mr. Henry?"

"Beautifully. I can't tell the difference. Hope you can. Where do you want me to bring 'em?"

"Downtown?"

"I can do that."

"Today?"

"Ummm, three hours."

"Good. I'll have a check for ten."

"This is a cash business."

"My check isn't any good?"

"No check is any good."

A silence. "Alright. I'll see you when you get here."

"See you then."

She was composed when I stepped back in. "Who was that?" she asked.

"None of your business. But it was your husband."

"Fuck him and fuck you."

"I think you've pushed the old horse a little too hard."

"I think you should stay out of my business."

"But you made it mine."

"I don't think so."

"It's a two-way street here, honey. Art Lewis's money? It's not up to me to protect it from thieves. Even if they wear diamonds and robes. But you killed a friend of mine. And for that, you pay."

"I'll deliver the killer."

"Fine. You'll deliver the killer and then you'll walk away from the money."

"I won't walk away from the money."

"I'll make you walk."

Then her phone rang. *E. Huff.* What the fuck did he want?

I pointed toward the front porch. "You can take it out there."

Ed Huff was in meltdown. His fear was contagious and Harry felt like he'd swallowed a package of stool softeners.

"The guy threatened me," whined Huff. "Said he's going to fuck with my license. Said the body was missing a toe! That he'd been dead for three days! That true? Was Lewis missing a toe?"

On TV, when the bad guys were closing in, Hangin' Harry's voice dropped an octave and little old ladies all over the country clutched their fistful of Kleenex and settled in for some old-time justice. But now he was just Harry Glidden, an old man with a bad back, an enlarged prostate, liver spots he hadn't lasered away, papilloma hanging from his perineum, an alienated family, some European cars he couldn't afford, and a sinkhole of debt on the beach. In poker terms, a handful of shit.

Who would call Huff? Fucking Bernardo, that's who. Bernardo the Incurious. This was Ellen's fault. Evil witch. "Look, Ed," he said, in his TV-justice voice, "just settle down. Everything's under control. You're not going to lose your license. Everything you did was legal and aboveboard. Wasn't it?"

"Uhh, yes. Of course it was."

"Then don't worry. There're always toads under rocks." Were toads found under rocks? Wouldn't they get squished? "Meanwhile,

I'll get on the horn over here and I'll tell you what. Call Ellen and tell her every detail you can remember."

"Call your wife?"

Put that way, thought Glidden, it sounded like he'd punted. "Not to make a report, Ed. Tell her the details because someone called her, *too.* Get it?"

"Someone called her, too?"

"Yes."

"What are you going to do?"

He was going to play with his pud, that's what. "Ed, get a hold of yourself. Don't ask me what I'm going to do. Just rest assured I'm going to do it." He'd play with his pud with *both* hands. "Now, go call Ellen."

He hung up.

Something bubbled in his colon and he got up and hurried for the can.

"Ellen?" said Huff. "This is Ed Huff."

"Well, hi, Ed." She tapped her foot, looking around. She'd never liked Laurel Canyon. That bullshit hippie granola peace vibe. "What can I do for you?"

"Uhh, actually I'm having some trouble and Harry said you were having some, too."

What kind of shit had Harry dumped her way? "This is very thoughtful of you, Ed. Harry's having trouble getting it up. Are you having that kind of problem, too?"

"Getting it, uh, uh, *what did you say?*"

"Never mind, Ed. Tell me what's up."

"I assure you I'm perfectly well."

"I'm glad for you. Why did you call?"

"A man called me up, threatened me. About Art Lewis."

Fucking Bernardo. This was a problem. "What kind of man?"

"I don't know. Mean, vicious. A criminal. A blackmailer. Said he cut a toe off the corpse."

"What *kind* of man was he, Ed. Did he speak with an accent?"

"No."

"And when did he call?"

"Forty minutes ago."

Did that mean it *wasn't Bernardo*? What had Bobby done? Was Bobby running a side game? How would he get Huff's number? But numbers could be had. She'd gotten Dick Henry's address easily enough. "This is important, Ed. Tell me every word you can remember he said."

Stressed-out Huff couldn't remember a thing. She had him go over it several times. Then a quote popped out. "I asked him who he was and he said, 'This is someone who's going to fuck up your party big-time.'"

Fuck up your party big-time. Where had she heard those exact words?

Then she remembered. At the church. Where the wrong woman had been commended to the arms of the Lord. Who said those words?

Dick Henry.

"I'll talk to you later, Ed. Thank you." Rage rolled over her skin like an electrical charge. Then horror. Bobby had been sent to see Bernardo. She dialed Bobby. Bobby wasn't picking up.

She threw open the door, stalked inside.

The murderess didn't look good. "Bad call?"

"I just talked to Ed Huff."

"How is Ed?"

"You should know."

"Should I?"

"You didn't just call him?"

"Who's Ed Huff?"

200

"Don't play fucking games with me, Dick Henry. You're the one who cut Art Lewis's toe off."

"*What?*" I summoned all my acting skills.

"The gasman always rings twice, Dick-Dave. I should have known."

"I don't know what you're talking about."

"Yes, you do, you stupid fuck." She laughed, victorious. "My sister would like you."

"Your sister's married."

"Not anymore, Dick-Dave." She picked up her purse. "And you can shove that toe up your ass for all the good it will do you now. You think your word, with your record, will stand up against Harry Glidden's? Or Ed Huff's? The death cert will stand. A missing toe? That must have happened when you cut it off at the funeral home." She pointed toward the kitchen. "Maybe someone will find it in your freezer. Which would be a Class A felony. Hope you don't end up in front of Hangin' Harry."

"You must think that toe was my only card," I bluffed. "You're not going to get away with this."

"It's over, Dick." Her laugh was cruel and hard, a double handful of silver dollars rolling down marble steps. "And you could've just shut up and got paid. And got laid, too. But, no. You get caught the way all chiselers do—trying to go straight. Stupid motherfucker."

With that, she left. My tabloid moment with a movie star had concluded. The fact that there was another woman smarter than Dick Henry didn't surprise me. They were everywhere.

There was a bright side. Though it felt tarnished in the moment. I would go collect ten thousand dollars from her husband. But only after I dealt with Art Lewis's fifth anterior digit.

CHAPTER FORTY-TWO

Big Red Lollipop

She was driving like a maniac, she knew that. What had Bobby done to Bernardo? The same thing he had done to Violet Brown? She parked her Mercedes behind Musso & Frank's, got a ticket from the smirking Mexicans. She restrained the urge to run. There was no reason to run. He had or he hadn't.

Bobby let her in and, immediately, here came questions about Bernardo. He wasn't in a mood to be badgered, for chrissake. "I don't talk about shit like that on a cell phone, bitch." He pointed toward the couch. "Sit down and shut up. I thought you told me he was the man."

"Bobby, what did you do?"

He held up the vial, examined it. "Can't you see I'm working here?"

Now he looked over at her. "I thought you told me Bernardo was the guy. Didn't you tell me that?"

"Yes."

"DIDN'T YOU TELL ME THAT?"

"Yes."

"And you *asked* me to scare the shit out of him, am I right?"

"Yes."

"But now you think he's innocent. GREAT." Bobby troweled off two pipes, slid one across the table. "Well, there's nothing for guilt like good crack cocaine." He slid a lighter over.

"What happened with Bernardo?"

Bobby lit up, exhaled the exquisite purpleness. "Bernardo's alright. I left him in the arms of his wife and children."

"He's safe?"

"Besides living in a rat-infested firetrap, he is."

"You son of a bitch, Bobby." Cool relief ran through her veins.

"Just light up your crack pipe, Mrs. Glidden."

She felt her face twisting into a smile. She inhaled slowly, perfectly.

"So you fucked Dick Henry, right?"

"Dick Henry cut off Art Lewis's toe. And no, I didn't fuck him. Not that it's your business."

"Where's the funeral going to be held?"

"Blessed Sacrament."

Bobby nodded. "Right across from Sunset Sound." Where the Doors had recorded their first album.

"Didn't you do some stuff there?"

"Yeah. Couple of things." Not "Crystal Ship" or "Soul Kitchen" quality, of course. But "Big Red Lollipop" wasn't meant for the same audience. Too bad he had compromised with that witless producer on "Black Candy." A string section! It would have been a surefire hit. Oh, well. Jim Morrison did his thing, Bobby Lebow had done his. Who was laughing now? He lit up, exhaled.

"Bobby?"

"I know that tone of voice. Don't ruin my buzz."

"There's one more loose end."

Of course. Of fucking course.

CHAPTER FORTY-THREE

Bambi Service

The toe was a relatively simple matter. Though I didn't have the Tarantino-Keitel African-American Disposal Service at my beck and call.

I did have Bambi.

Bambi was a stone alcoholic and my next-door neighbor. One day, after a party, I saw her in my backyard. She was knocking over beer cans and licking up the beer. Pretty soon she was staggering around and then she fell asleep on the grass.

Did I mention Bambi was a poodle?

Well, half a poodle. The other half was Labrador. Which made her a Labradoodle. That detestable appellation alone demanded alcohol or a bullet. But, not possessing opposable thumbs, therefore incapable of pulling a trigger, Bambi, festooned with wilted, greasy ribbons, drank out of wretched embarrassment.

I filled one side of a double doggie-dish with Budweiser, Bambi's favorite, and called her over the fence. "Come here, girl," I said in friendly fashion. She wagged her tail, looked down, sidled right over. You always sidle for your enabler. I rubbed her head.

In the other side was Art Lewis's microwaved toe and part of an Angus burger from McDonald's. Don't read Upton Sinclair.

With alacrity and gratitude Bambi lapped up the beer, then

lay down to gnaw on the toe in the sun. If I didn't know better, I would've sworn she winked at me as I left.

I picked up the paintings from Dennis, put them back to back in a cardboard flat, and drove downtown. The judge's secretary, Arnelle, met me downstairs and ushered me along the back way to Glidden's office.

"Hello, Mr. Henry." The judge stuck out his hand, we shook. Every inch an officer of the court.

"How've you been, Judge? How goes justice?"

"I've been fine. And justice is the fruit of vigilance. We work at it every day." He flashed his veneers at me.

I felt that tingle in my fist.

"Any difficulties in *your mission,* Mr. Henry?"

"None." Carefully I removed one of the paintings, showed it to him front and back, set it on the black leather couch. Then I took the other one out, did the same.

Glidden came close, studied them, shook his head.

"Which is which?"

I laughed. "You're the expert, Judge."

He looked sharply at me. "You *do* know?"

"Of course."

The judge peered at them again. Rubbed his thumb over a corner. Then over the corner of the other. But Dennis Donnelly was a textural genius.

"It's money time, Judge."

He nodded, went to his desk, removed a white envelope, handed it to me. I counted out a hundred hundreds. Ten stacks of ten.

"Thanks, Judge."

"Thank *you,* Mr. Henry." He looked again at his pictures. "I can't tell the difference. You *do* know?"

"I do know." And, of course, the judge knew, too.

For the third time he studied the paintings. Then he pointed to the one I'd first put on the couch. "This is the one."

I nodded. "That's it. You got it. But how did you know?"

"You really can't tell?"

"Not by looking. There's a piece of tape on the back."

Glidden turned it over, thumbed the mark he had put there before giving it to me. Dennis Donnelly and I had inspected the work thoroughly. "This an accident here?" asked Dennis, pointing to a screwdriver dent in the framing.

"There are no accidents in the world," was my reply.

I watched the judge study the canvas. I don't know if he looked older or younger. But his face softened as he stared at it.

"How did you know, Judge?"

Glidden looked at Henry, the Shortcut Man. What was it to be insensitive to art? How did one walk through the halls of life? Through relentless fields of the ordinary, the prosaic, and the profane. The shallow Shortcut Man probably didn't read books, either. Probably read "graphic novels." Which were fucking comic books, come on. Comic books and gum, his mother's anathema.

"How do I know what's real? It's a feeling I get, Mr. Henry." He indicated his choice. "This moves me. Almost to tears. Above and beyond its visual beauty. It moves me somehow. But this one"—he pointed to the second—"this one leaves me cold. I don't feel anything."

I nodded, chastened.

He persisted. "You don't feel anything? Nothing?"

I looked at both, shook my head. Nothing. I felt nothing. "To me, they're exactly identical, Judge."

He smiled, sorry for me.

I left him with his treasures.

Minus ten thousand dollars.

CHAPTER FORTY-FOUR

Erin Secures Her Due

The more she thought about it, the more Erin Halle was angry. Which was a little too polite. She was pissed. She had been deprived of a husband, and that had been a very important part of a big deal.

True, she had not been imprisoned for what really should not be considered a crime, but the marriage to rich Arthur, which she surely could have turned to her advantage, had not taken place. Certainly, if she had backed out, they would have been furious.

There had been a time when no one could resist her charm. And when the prime of her physical beauty had passed, she had her formidable skills as an actress to rely on. She still had those skills.

And those skills would be there the day her infatuation with cocaine came to its natural conclusion. Because everything had a natural conclusion. But she wasn't ready yet. Not quite yet. She took a second hit on the pipe. It was mostly residue but she could no longer afford the profligacy she had once enjoyed.

She had called Ellen Havertine and lodged her complaint about dead Arthur. Rich, dead Arthur. Yes, avoiding jail was a blessing, of course it was, but their were other benefits she had every right to expect. No, this wasn't blackmail, it was a statement of fact. Taking a moment to compare and contrast. In any case, in the least case, she deserved a little more than a handshake and a fuck-off. She had been more than ready to uphold her end of the bargain.

And finally Ellen, who was really shit as an actress, saw sense. Would Erin accept forty thousand dollars? Forty? She was hoping for six figures. Well, said Ellen, six figures was a possibility down the line. But forty was today money.

She had settled for today money. Because it wasn't a dream. It was money *today*. A messenger. Bobby who? Bobby Lebow? *That* Bobby Lebow, really. Okay, then. And she hoped she hadn't been too forward in making this call. It was just if a person had rights, they had rights. Thank you, Ellen, you're a darling. And I've always loved your work. Inspiring work. Goodbye.

She looked down into the small, carved wooden box where she kept her shit. If she didn't know better, someone was stealing from her. Here in her own house! Down to her last gram. She broke off a big, celebratory hunk, stuffed it into the pipe.

An anticipatory gust of pleasure and well-being rolled over her body as she stared out the window down on Los Angeles. How bad could things be? She was free, she lived high above the city, she was in mid-career, today was money day, and soon she would renounce the cool hand of sweet cousin cocaine. As the Stones had put it. Loved the Stones.

A banging gradually resolved into a knock at the door. Already? She looked at clock. Had two hours passed since she talked to the judge-marrying shrew? It had.

She opened the door and immediately recognized Bobby Lebow.

"Hi, Erin," said Bobby.

"Hi, Bobby." Bobby wasn't much of actor. He had survived on personality. But it took all kinds. "Come in." Now she remembered. He'd been caught explaining cunnilingus to a producer's fourteen-year-old daughter in his trailer. The girl was head of his fan club. Or something. A little knob-doctor.

She led Bobby back to the breakfast nook, where they sat.

"We did a few things together, didn't we?" Bobby smiled his trademark smirk.

"We did," said Erin. "I played your aunt who came to visit and had to play bass in your band for a night."

"The show must go on."

"We lip-synched to a dreadful little tune."

"You have a really good memory."

"And I remember the song. 'Black Candy.' Wow. Do you remember that song? It was awful." She sang a bit of it, "Black ca-a-a-andy."

"Of course I remember it. I wrote it."

Erin burst out laughing. "You didn't."

"I did."

"No, you didn't."

"Yes, I did." He sang the chorus in its entirety.

A silence followed.

Ellen felt color rise into her face. "I'm so sorry."

"Don't be. It sucked." Then they both laughed.

"Did you bring me something, Bobby?"

He smiled. "I brought you two things." From his jacket he brought out a thick envelope. "Forty Gs, in hundreds." He slid the envelope across the table.

She reached forward, took possession of the envelope, brought it slowly back across the table. Relief. Now it was *hers*. Now she could pay Mr. Rigrod. Uhh, well, she'd give him a taste. At an ounce of cocaine a week, she had a six-month run in front of her. Glorious. "What else do you have?"

He pulled a leather case out of another pocket. He unzipped it. Inside was a plastic Ziploc. Inside the Ziploc were two liquor-spout pipes and a little bag of white rocks.

Oh, good Lord. She could taste it already.

He grinned, loaded the pipes. "I'm told we share a vice or two."

She looked down at the rocks. "I guess we do."

He slipped one of the pipes across the table. "Bon appetit."

Her hand closed on the pipe. "And bon appetit, to you, too, sir."

Yesss. The taste was wonderful and clean. She exhaled and the pleasure wave hit her. She nodded at Bobby. "This tastes really good. Really good."

"It is really good," he replied. "Let me refill you." He did so. "I love the taste, too. To me, it tastes purple. Does it taste purple to you?"

She nodded. Purple. In fact, that's exactly what it tasted like . . . almost. "I would say lavender. Lavender."

He reached for her pipe. In his leather case was another, smaller bag of rocks. He broke off a chunk, pushed it into the end of her pipe. He refilled his from the little pile on the table. He slid Erin's across the table to her. "Bon voyage."

She took the pipe. How useful it would be to know Bobby Lebow. "Thanks, Bobby. How good to see you again."

"The pleasure is all mine," he said, raising his pipe in salute.

She returned the gesture, then lit up. Something struck her immediately. It wasn't purple. "Funny taste," she said, looking at Bobby.

Bobby inhaled the purple. The violet. The lavender. The indigo.

He watched Erin Halle. She was in distress. The poison had crossed the blood-brain barrier as quickly as the cocaine would have. Already she had lost the ability to breathe, now her eyes started to bug out. She leaned back, arching slowly but desperately in her chair, eyes on the ceiling, the muscles in her throat standing out like cords.

Then it was over. She was dead. Frozen.

Bobby picked up the money envelope, got his shit together, checked around one more time.

He walked to the sink, got a sponge, wet it, wiped down the side of the table where he'd been sitting. Finished, he tossed the sponge across the room into the sink.

Using the sleeve of his jacket, he opened Erin's front door, walked out into the night.

Want a job done right, do it yourself.

PART THREE

Public Property

CHAPTER FORTY-FIVE

Sometimes the Bad Guys Win

I was feeling low that night. Though the triumph of evil was not unprecedented, it remained depressing. The Glidden plan seemed destined to succeed. Somewhere, in a pile of shit, was what remained of Lewis's toe.

Then Rojas knocked at the door. The Mayan prince always cheered me up. He studied my face, found it lacking. "Fuck you," he said, sparking his chronic.

I discussed the Art Lewis situation with him. He shook his head. "Dude. If the bad guys don't win sometimes, when the good guys win it wouldn't be shit." He took a deep draft. "Don't take things so personal." He exhaled and a thought struck him. "You could always lean on the judge. That could be a payday."

"But that makes me a partner." I couldn't get Violet Brown out of my mind. She was not collateral damage.

"Well, you could stand up at the funeral and tell the story," said Rojas, "get arrested and shit, spend the night in the can."

I didn't want to spend the night in the can. What I needed was Art Lewis to tell his *own* story.

I drank a reflective beer as the prince banked a couple more thoughtful tokes, leaned back into the couch. Then he had a request. "Tell me, again, about the border guard and the smuggler dude."

I guess.

"Come on, Dick-Dave, tell me." Rojas snorted. *"Dick-Dave."*

The story, which I loved, seemed to illustrate some facet of human behavior. It went like this.

Every day, at the border, a man came across on a bicycle carrying a small box of sand. This went on for twenty-five years. Finally, it was the border guard's last day on the job. He had sifted the sand every single day, found nothing. So he made a request of the bicyclist. "Look. I know you're smuggling something. I *know* it. Now, today is my last day. I retire tomorrow. I'll never tell anyone. I don't care. But I've got to know. Tell me what you're smuggling."

The bicyclist tipped his hat. "Bicycles," he said.

"Bicycles," said Rojas weakly, laughing, hands on his belly, shaking his head in wonder and gratification.

Then, *bingo,* it hit me. The last-chance idea to bring down the Gliddens.

It was preposterous. It was ridiculous. It was ludicrous. But it just might work.

CHAPTER FORTY-SIX

Operation Lazarus

Art Lewis's funeral had been scheduled for one o'clock Saturday afternoon at Blessed Sacrament Church on Sunset. Bill Hadderson, senior driver for McKinley Brothers, rolled out in the 2008 Cadillac hearse at 10:45 for an 11:30 delivery at the church. As senior driver he had pick of the services. Today there would be a three-figure tip. Maybe four. In the rearview mirror, he adjusted his face from its natural crafty avarice into one of solemn compassion. Then some asshole cut in front of him on Union Street and he had to slam on his brakes to avoid a collision. Adding insult to injury, at the stoplight the interloper was sitting through a red light.

Hadderson laid on the horn. Come on, asshole.

But asshole didn't come on. In fact, asshole got out of his car and walked back toward him. He was a stocky Hispanic man in Wayfarers and a black leather porkpie hat. Hadderson didn't take shit as a matter of course. He rolled down his window. "What the fuck, buddy?"

Then he noticed Porkpie had a gun.

"Slide on over, *tio,*" said Rojas, "and you won't get hurt."

Hadderson found his tongue, the acerbic, saberlike delight of the Clown Room, strangely thick and incapable of speech. Then another man got in on the passenger side.

"This is Señor Tavo Gonzalez," said Porkpie, formally. "If you behave, Señor Gonzalez will release you and give you five of these," he showed Hadderson some hundred-dollar bills, "for your trouble. Neither you, your vehicle, or your passenger will be hurt in any way. Do you understand?"

Ideas of valor passed jerkily through Hadderson's mind but didn't add up to a plan of action. To fight for the dead increasingly seemed a labored cause, far from the immediacy of life. His bladder was full. "I understand," said Hadderson.

"Good," said Porkpie, handing him a blindfold. "Put this on."

Blessed Sacrament Church had a capacity of fourteen hundred souls, including the side chapel and the children's room. About eight hundred souls were in attendance for the Art Lewis ceremony. The hearse had arrived twenty minutes late, and it seemed an older model than the death of an important man might suggest.

In fact, thought Harry Glidden, that thing isn't even a Cadillac. It's a fucking Pontiac! Who the fuck ordered a Pontiac? An *old* Pontiac? You didn't want your final journey in economy class. When you died with an extra fifty mil in your back pocket, you wanted Cadillac. He would raise hell with McKinley later.

The casket was A-1, however. Bronze, shiny, and guaranteed to withstand the pressure of six feet of heavy earth. It was laden thickly with roses and accompanied by a double brace of Hispanics. Hispanics added a nice slice of native solemnity. The leader seemed to be a stocky man in black suit wearing very dark Wayfarers. Was he going to wear those sunglasses inside the church?

Apparently, he was.

In the choir loft, under a wide expanse of stained glass, Clifford Spence, the best funeral organist in Los Angeles, presided over an Allen "Elite," the finest of all domestically produced organs. He and the Allen had played for the Pontiff on the supreme prelate's last visit to the United States. Maybe he would be invited to the Vatican. Let his fingers do the walking. *Clifford Spence at the Vatican. One night only.* He leaned into Bach's "Jesu, Joy of Man's Desiring."

As the sequences rose and fell beneath his fingers, Spence turned to study his lone companion in the loft, a man looking down on the congregation. Though the man wore a black suit with Roman collar, his vibe was not ecclesiastical. Spence couldn't put a finger on it.

The organist was looking at me. I smiled, raised a hand, blessed him: *In nomine Patri, et filii, et spiritus sancti.* Something like that.

Showtime.

An audible wave ran through the throng as the flowered casket was rolled up the central aisle, four men of honor on each side. From the floor, toward the rear, Rojas turned, signaled up to me.

I nodded in reply. All was in order.

At the stroke of one, bells tolled and a young priest mounted the pulpit. The congregation hushed by degrees, finally a few coughs, then silence. "Ladies and gentlemen, His Honor, Harold J. Glidden."

I watched Harry Glidden, murderer, make his way from the first pew on the left to the pulpit. The judge cleared his throat, looked out over his audience, then began to speak in his famous baritone.

"Art Lewis was a friend of mine." A long pause. "He was a builder. He was a fighter. He was a thinker. He was a reader. He was a sailor. He was a dancer. He rode a Harley. He was a man's man. And he was a woman's man."

In the first pew Eileen Klasky, in black widow's weeds and veil, stifled a tragic sob.

"Art Lewis lived. Art Lewis *lived*. And he was an example of life well lived. He was a great, great human being."

And so on and so on.

That and other cut-rate encomiums wafted up through the afternoon heat as a long parade of celebrated, sanctimonious half-wits climbed to the pulpit. Robert Patrick, Nedra's persecutor, introduced himself. Art had some compassionate finger in the Azure Gardens pie. Art cared deeply for something or other. Was committed to it. Lived for it. Died for it.

The show went on. Art Lewis was a nice guy, Puss had told me so, but these professional ass-lickers pegged him somewhere between George Washington and Mother Teresa. He had chopped down the cherry tree, true—but only in order to construct a artful crucifix for the visual edification of the starving.

Finally Nursie, heavy with grief, every step an ordeal, made the ascent.

"Hi." Some snuffling. "T-thanks for coming." Sniffling. "I . . . I loved Art so much. He was . . . he was such a man. Such a *man*. He was kind. He was, uh, generous."

What else might she say about a man she'd never known?

"He was, uh, he was . . . many things. He was fair, he was . . . he was tall. He was a tall man."

He was *tall*. Maybe she meant *tall* allegorically. But, fuck it, I'd heard as much as I could without puking. It was time to disrupt the circus and alarm the citizens. I pulled out my phone and dialed.

"Hello?" said a whispering voice.

"Commence Operation Lazarus."

"Commence Operation Lazurus, aye." In the Navy, exact repetition of an order was called verbatim compliance.

Meanwhile Nursie-at-the-pulpit continued the ramble and bamble. "Art was far-seeing."

No shit. He was tall.

Then a loud thud was heard.

If some of the nearby churchgoers didn't know better, the sound seemed to emanate from the casket. But maybe it was the acoustics and the PA system.

Nursie had paused, but now resumed. "Art was far-seeing and he—"

Two loud thuds. A few roses fell off the casket. Heads turned.

Nursie, unaware of the source of the interruption, and finding no orders on the face of her sister, soldiered on. "He was far-seeing and he saw far. One time Art said to me—"

Now a muffled shout was heard. Followed instantly by a scream from a pew close to the casket. All heads rotated toward the casket and a buzz rolled through the congregation. An older woman, holding her veiled hat to her head, hurried out, dragging her hapless husband.

In a seat toward the rear, where less-important mourners were to be found, a half-smile, quickly extinguished, passed over the face of Pussy Grace. She remembered Dick's odd command. *Go to the funeral and enjoy.* Enjoy?

Nursie struggled on. "Is everything okay?"

Now a voice was clearly audible. "Lemme out of here!" With more bangs and blows. Then, to wide horror, the lid of the casket rose a few inches before falling shut with a metallic clang.

Nursie hung desperately on to the pulpit.

In the face of the miracle, fear spread like gas through the church. There was a controlled yet concerted movement for the exits.

"Lemme out of here!" cried the voice. Again the casket opened and fell shut.

Then, with a roar and a mighty push, the casket was thrown open entirely. The pleasant effluvium of well-spoiled meat rushed into the room.

This was all it took. The congregation abandoned all order in a frantic, roiling, heaving drive for the light of day. Shrieks, hollers, imprecations, and cries to God could be heard amidst the running, the shoving, and the trampling. But Blessed Sacrement had only four exits, one on each side and the main doors toward the rear, so a great stacking-up occurred. A *bullop,* I mused. A Navy definition. Ten pounds of shit in a five-pound bag.

Then, and only then, casket gaping, did Rutland Atwater, hair dyed white, face black with apparent rot, sit up, grinning in his funeral suit, the man whose time had come.

"Where is my wife?" shouted the dead man, climbing out of his eternal resting place with rotting hands. "Where is beautiful Eileen?"

But Eileen was crawling toward the sacristy on her hands and knees, as her legs had lost the power to assist her in their normal fashion.

By this time the dead man had fully resurrected and walked the earth, arms outstretched like a TV mummy. "Where is my beautiful wife?" he shouted, "and where is my toe? Who cut off my toe?"

In the church parking lot, fourteen accidents took place, and it was claimed by some that the mummy, laughing, had commandeered the Pontiac hearse and disappeared down Sunset Boulevard in the direction of the Whisky a Go Go.

CHAPTER FORTY-SEVEN

A Hit Before She Split

Forty minutes later, in apartment 3G, Bobby opened the door, admitting Ellen Glidden.

"That motherfucker! That motherfucker!"

Bobby was in the middle of cooking up a few grams. "What motherfucker?" He swirled the vial around.

"Dick Henry, that *son of a bitch*. He ruined everything. The funeral was a disaster." She was almost crying with rage. "A fucking disaster."

"I think I heard something on the radio. There was a miracle, right? The Jesuits raised the dead?"

"It isn't fucking funny, Bobby."

Bobby poured off the water and let two sludgy boogers roll out on top of *Art Pepper Meets the Rhythm Section*. "Raising the dead on Sunset Boulevard has elements of humor to it. Where's Bob Hope when you need him?" He snickered. "But he was dead three years before he was dead."

"This isn't fucking funny, Bobby. You know what this means?"

Bobby lit up, exhaled. Here was a small miracle. On Cherokee Avenue, for fuck's sake. Crack cocaine would combust even before it was dry. "Listen, bitch, I know what it better *not* mean. It better not mean, *Bobby, I'm so sorry. Bobby, I fucking apologize.* I don't give a fuck what went wrong. I did my part. You promised me a million dollars and I want my million dollars. And that's it."

"What's it?"

"I want my million dollars. You promised and there's no going back. Or I go to the fucking cops." He filled his pipe again, lit up.

"Fuck you, Bobby."

"Fine, Ellen. But you got a lot farther to fall than I do. *Mrs. Glidden.*"

He refilled and lit up one more time. The pleasure rolled through him, perfectly, evenly, spherically, completely. Whatever happened to him, whatever price he would come to pay, he wouldn't complain. It was worth it. It was worth it.

"Are you *threatening* me, Bobby?"

"What would you call it?" Out of the corner of his eye he saw his revolver. On the bottom level of the coffee table. He reached for it, slid it across the table.

"Yes, I'm threatening you. And I'm giving you a solution at the same time. But you don't have the guts."

From a small bag of rocks in his leather case, he filled a second pipe and slid it across the table. "And here's a little courage, too."

Ellen picked up the gun, hefted it. Form and function comprised a perfect heaviness. On the table her phone vibrated. *Harry.* Weak-sister Harry. And now all the shit, all the shit that would come down. Well, she would deal with it. Sort things out. Because that's what she did. Some people did things, figured things through, made decisions. Others sat around puling and whining.

Her arm straightened and, as if of its own accord, the weapon pointed itself at Bobby's head.

"I'm sick of you, Bobby. You're a leech and you've been sucking off me for fifteen years. I'm cutting you loose."

"Fuck if you are." He lit up and the purple kingdom was his.

"We're through, Bobby."

Bobby, supremely unfazed, looked up at the gun, exhaled. He refilled his pipe, reached for his Bic. "You don't have the guts."

The Glock 17 had a muzzle velocity of eight hundred feet per second. Meaning Bobby was dead in forty-five thousandths of a second. The pipe fell from his fingers, dark red blood welled up from the small hole in the exact center of his forehead.

What did she feel? Nothing. She felt nothing. Step-on-a-bug nothing. The sound of the gun hadn't been that loud either. She went to the filthy sink, wiped off the gun with some 409 and a paper towel. Just like the criminals did on *Special Counsel.* Perfect. No prints.

She laid the gun on the coffee table, grabbed up her purse and coat. Then she saw the pipe that Bobby had prepared for her. That fragrance filled her mind. Of course, a last hit. A hit before she split. No, she shouldn't. But why the fuck not? Dead Bobby wouldn't object.

She set purse and coat aside, sat down, lit up.

But the taste—what was this shit?

She couldn't seem to draw breath. She arched her back in her effort, saw the yellow bulb hanging from the ceiling . . . and then she . . .

CHAPTER FORTY-EIGHT

A Gray Kitten with One Eye

The early news on Channel 9 allowed me to relive the resurrection I had fomented. Apparently, with the exception of Lazarus, Paul McCartney, and Jesus Himself, something unique had been achieved. Certainly in modern times. Ted Sargent did not mention my name.

But victory left me restless. Kiyoko maintained her intransigence and time hung heavy on my hands. I decided I would head down to Bledsoe and get it over with.

Nedra answered her phone on the fourth ring. I told her something important had come up. Robert Patrick's appearance had reminded me directly.

As important as the resurrection in Hollywood?

I professed ignorance and was believed.

She'd made a pot of coffee and poured me a cup.

"So, how are things going? Latrell told me Mr. Ket had put a lid on the intimidation aspect down here."

Nedra sat back, studied me. "Mr. Ket is a five-star phony. I don't think he's set a single foot in Africa."

She was right, of course. I'd met Bosto Ket in his loose role as a Nigerian prince. Kufi, dashiki, an accent from somewhere. We had embarked upon a shortcut adventure but, during a surveillance interlude, Bosto had stepped on a nail. Without thought, he had given voice to a florid stream of expletives in Brooklynese.

I looked over at him. "If I didn't know better, Bosto, I'd say you were from New York."

Bosto swept off his kufi and threw it on the floor. "I'm from Crown Heights, Dick. And I miss it."

"It's not a man's name that's important," I paraphrased. "It's the content of his character."

Bosto took a deep breath, explained. "My name is Nile Benson. Which served me well enough in the Navy. But after I was out for a while, and things weren't going so good, I thought that maybe I'd just start over."

"And you saw that Eddie Murphy movie."

Bosto grinned. "I did see it." He took off shoe and sock, squeezed a little blood out of the puncture. "My girlfriend had just kicked me out. She lived in El Segundo. I was driving home in the rain. Marine Avenue. Manhattan Beach. I forget what year it was but it was a hell of a winter and we had six or seven straight days of rain. In town I passed a business and some of the sign had shorted out. And that's where I saw my new name, my future." Bosto picked up his kufi, slapped the dust off of it, put it back on his head.

"What business was that?" I guess I was slow on the uptake.

"Boston Market."

BOSTON MARKET
BOSTO   KET

Thusly, a Nigerian prince entered the universe. "What do you want me to call you, Bosto? Bosto? Or should it be Nile?"

"Call me . . ." Here he paused, if not at the Rubicon, at least the East River. "Call me . . ."

"Why don't I call you Bosto? That's how we met. That'll keep things simple."

Bosto grinned, we shook hands, had enjoyed each other's company ever since.

"Where's Bosto from, Dick?" asked Nedra. "Did he say?"

"Nigeria. But maybe it's Gambia." I shrugged.

"Nigeria, Gambia, all the same to you," said Nedra, parsing her displeasure. "Now why are you here?"

I looked deep into her dark eyes. "Business. I've been asked to ask you a question."

"By whom?"

"By the man building Azure Gardens."

"You're a traitor."

"I'm a businessman."

"What does he want, Dick?"

"He wants to know why you're insisting on staying here. Bledsoe Park."

Anger narrowed her eyes. "Do I really have to explain a black woman's connection—"

"A black person's connection to the land and all that stuff."

"All that black-tragedy stuff."

"I'm not going there. I'm appealing to your intellect. Bledsoe is doomed. Azure Gardens is coming. You must know that. You must see that. It can't be stopped. Why are you holding on?"

"Why don't you leave, Dick."

I pressed on. "Mr. Patrick has offered you a hundred thousand dollars. This place, on the tax rolls, is worth eighty-two fifty. Why are you holding on?"

"Get the hell out of here, Dick Henry."

"I've heard you talk about schools and clinics and after-school programs. Cash money would give you an opportunity to do all those things."

Nedra took a deep breath, exhaled as if she were concentrating her essence. "This woman won't be pushed off her land."

"Not for a hundred grand."

She held her forehead in her right hand, looked down at the table-top. Her voice was a whisper. "Not for a . . . for a measly hundred grand."

"Okay. For a measly two hundred?"

"Two hundred?"

"Two hundred thousand dollars. Is that enough?"

She looked up at me. "No. It's not enough."

"Okay. Three. Three hundred thousand. Is that enough?"

I saw her eyes fill with tears. "No," she said. Like there was a nail in her guts. "It's not enough."

Her little gray, one-eyed kitty took that moment to run through the kitchen. He looked at me, scuttled behind the refrigerator. In that instant, all was revealed to me.

"Four. What about four hundred thousand, Nedra?"

Tears overflowed and ran down her cheeks. "No, Dick. I can't do it. *Can't do it.*" Her hands were knotted together and she lowered her head, between her arms, facedown, to the tabletop.

"And what about *five*?" I knew what her answer would be.

Nedra sobbed as if her heart would break. "No, Dick, no. *I can't.*"

I checked a final time. Just for drill. Or perhaps the Shortcut Man was getting a small, hard, cruel piece of his own. "A *million* dollars, Nedra. A million. What do you say to that?"

She groaned a terrible groan from the bottom of her soul.

But I'd had enough. It was time.

"Why don't you tell me, Nedra?" I said quietly. "Tell me who's under the house."

Nedra raised her head up, looked at me through centuries of pain. Then she lowered her head back to the tabletop, and the torrent was loosed.

I put my hand on her shoulder.

Her brother, she later explained, was under the house. Under a thick layer of home-laid concrete. Poured by her father. Her brother had come home very high, disappointed and enraged with something that had gone wrong. An argument had broken out with his father. The argument had turned violent. It had been the culmination of years of argument and her father had only meant to wave the gun.

Nedra had been trapped in the house ever since. For twenty years. Maintaining her deceased father's reputation and, by extension, polishing the urban legend that her brother had become. A brother taken down by the man.

The FBI and the CIA denied responsibility. But no one believed them. There were the Tuskeegee Airmen, after all. There was Rosewood. There was Emmett Till. There were a million horrors that had turned into statistics. Strange Fruit.

Not that Nedra disbelieved the precepts she proclaimed from Pulpit Bledsoe. She did believe them. But there was no choice as to her espousing those principles.

"What do I do, Dick?" A great weight had been lifted from her shoulders. In sharing, light had pierced the darkness.

I looked at her. "Obviously, the truth isn't going to be good for much of anything," I began.

Her solemn dark eyes regarded me. Then that melodious laugh bubbled out of her throat and she laughed and I laughed and we laughed. It was probably hysterical but we couldn't stop. Until tears began anew. "What do I do?"

"I'll think of something," I said. Because I would. Because I'm the Shortcut Man. And, suddenly, there it was in my mind.

CHAPTER FORTY-NINE

Public Property

Six months had passed and the morning was sunny and brisk, just the way I like it. My 1969 Cadillac Coupe de Ville, perfectly tuned, rolled down Sunset Boulevard on the way downtown.

Perfect justice is impossible but I had put matters in the ballpark.

Pussy Grace married Clark Peach and was now Pussy Peach. Excuse me, Penelope Peach.

Ellen Glidden had inhaled some kind of poison and Hangin' Harry had swallowed his gun.

Art's death had been reexamined by the coroner's office and certain questions had arisen concerning his late and surprising marriage. Various liars and prevaricators sought refuge in amended versions of the truth, and somewhere, I knew, an altar boy was taking it in the can for Almighty God. All was right with the world.

Commensurate with Art having died twice, a second funeral had been scheduled. It was extremely well attended, SRO, and a good time was had by all. Clifford Spence again presided from the choir loft. For a few minutes during the service I felt as if I knew the deceased. Art sounded like a nice guy, a man I would've liked. Happy trails, Mr. Lewis. May the road rise to meet your step.

Another rendition of the Lewis will was located. At the hearing, a platoon of cranks researching UFOs, reincarnation, alchemy,

231

reverse speech, automatic writing, remote viewing, ectoplasmic visitation, and ESP were surprised to encounter seven very blond, very busty women in their midst. Ranging from forty to sixty-five, Stormy, Kitty, Windy, Lola, Ginger, Lisa, and Lulu had apparently performed singular service on Art's behalf over the years and each received a hundred thousand dollars cash. Penelope Grafton was bequeathed five hundred thousand dollars.

Of which she gave me a generous 15 percent.

"You don't have to, Puss," I'd said.

"But I want to, Dick," she replied.

Well. Okay.

Upon reaching downtown Los Angeles I went south on Central Avenue. Bledsoe Park was a fading memory. Azure Gardens was in its infancy, but in full swing, large tracts of large Spanish-style homes rising from the fresh dark soil. But in the middle of this nascent paradise a park had been established, and that's where I was going.

The park was small, two hundred feet on a side. In the center of the park was a modest two-story house, now repaired and repainted, surrounded by a large green lawn and perfect, white picket fencing. A sign proclaimed the site was the historical home of Charles Ransom Scott, a man who stood up for truth, for justice, for all men. It was hoped he still might come back.

On the lawn, at the podium, stood three people. The mayor of Los Angeles, Mr. Robert Patrick, and Nedra Scott.

I missed the mayor's speech but he never said anything anyway.

Patrick was finishing up his remarks. Heroes arose with necessity. When Los Angeles needed Charles Ransom Scott, Charles Ransom Scott had stepped forward. And had paid the bitter price. This park would be an everlasting testimony to Ransom's belief in a better America.

Then Patrick introduced Nedra Scott. Nedra graciously thanked the mayor, thanked Mr. Patrick, thanked the people everywhere, but especially those of Bledsoe Park for keeping the memory and ideals of her brother alive. Alive here, right here, in the very home he had grown up in. A home to be preserved, untouched, for the ages. "We will meet here again when he returns," Nedra concluded. The crowd cheered. Nedra waved and stepped off the world stage.

I greeted her on the grass. She was relaxed and looked good.

"You're a good speaker," I said.

She nodded. "Thank you. And that's the last of it."

Latrell had come up by her side. We shook hands, small-talked. He was playing a little alto sax now.

"Eric Dolphy," said Dick Henry, jazz scholar. Of course, I didn't know anything about Dolphy. Wouldn't recognize a note of his music. Dolphy was Rojas's favorite artist.

"Didn't think you'd know about him," said Latrell.

"You'd be surprised what I know."

"What did you find out about my uncle?"

I shook my head. "Nothing more. I looked around. But nothing. Sorry."

"I think he's under the house," said Latrell.

Christ Jesus. Fibissedeh face tried to hang on. Tried to pretend he was thinking. I don't know if Latrell was fooled but Nedra had turned to me. "We gotta go."

I nodded, swallowed. "What are you going to do now?"

"Going to go live in Amsterdam for a while," said Nedra. "See what life is like on the other side of the world."

Sounded like a plan. Latrell eyed me. I hoped he wasn't as smart as his mother. But he probably was.

Nedra looked at me, into me, with her dark eyes, then stepped forward, hugged me long and strong. "Goodbye," she whispered, "Hud."

CHAPTER FIFTY

Kostabi #3

I found the Harbor Freeway and rolled north. At the 10 I headed west. For Pacific Palisades. Kiyoko had not called me, but I thought, the hell with it, I'll just go over there and tough it out.

I parked in front of her house, took the package from my backseat, walked to the doorbell, and rang.

Kiyoko opened up. Hand on hip, she looked skeptically at me. "Dick. What is it you want?"

Geez. I was nervous. "I have something for you."

My declaration didn't get me far. "Yes? What?"

My package was a large, flat rectangle. "A painting. I've brought you a painting."

"A painting? You?"

"Maybe you don't know the real me."

"Maybe I do."

"If you did you'd be missing me."

Kiyoko's eyes narrowed with distrust. "A painting?"

I opened the box, lifted it out, held it up for her.

Her eyes went wide. "Kostabi! *Kostabi?*"

I shrugged. "Of course it's a Kostabi. What am I, a barbarian?"

"I *love* Kostabi," she breathed.

Isn't that the purpose of art? To express what cannot be communicated in words? "This is for you," I said, handing it to her. *"Kostabi Number Five."*

She was awe-stricken, looked up me uncomprehendingly. "It looks . . . it looks real."

"It should look real. It is real."

It was real. Dennis Donnelly, now adrift in Mexico, had, at my further instruction, painted *two* phonies.

Kiyoko looked up into my face wonderingly. "You really care about me, don't you?"

Of course I did.

"Yes, dear, I do."

Two diamond tears rolled down her face and she reached up with her two tiny, perfect hands, placed one on each side of my unpretty face, and kissed me tenderly on the lips.

"Come into my home, Dick Henry," she said.

I smiled. "Okay."

I went in.

Hud.

Acknowledgments

Andrew C. Rigrod, Esq.

Paul Pompian

Ryan Harbage

Anna deVries

Thank you all for your support and encouragement.

Song lyrics courtesy of Pearly King, www.pearlykingmusic.com.

About the Author

p. g. sturges was born in Hollywood, California. Punctuated by fitful intervals of school, he has subsequently occupied himself as a submarine sailor, a Christmas tree farmer, a dimensional metrologist, a writer, and a musician.